Li Tong (1953-2004) was born in Hualien, Taiwan. Celebrated and vigorously studied in the Chinese-speaking world, his writings range across lyrics, essays, children's literature, fiction and drama. He won several prestigious literary awards in Taiwan, including a *National Arts Award* and a *Sun Yat-Sen Arts Award*. Over the decades, his writings have attracted a wide readership from the ordinary reader to students and academics, appearing in influential anthologies as well as on school and university reading lists. His novels have been adapted into radio plays and films. *Again I See the Gaillardias* is his first book to be translated into English.

Brandon Yen was educated in Taiwan, Scotland and England. He holds a PhD in English from the University of Cambridge. As well as writing and translating, he has a particular interest in practising botanical illustration. His translation of Li Tong's *Again I See the Gaillardias* was awarded a grant from the National Museum of Taiwan Literature.

Again I See
the Gaillardias

LI TONG

Again I See
the Gaillardias

Translated from the Chinese
by Brandon Yen

balestierpress

Balestier Press
71-75 Shelton Street, London WC2H 9JQ
www.balestier.com

Again I See the Gaillardias
Original title: 再見天人菊
Copyright © Li Tong, 1986
English translation copyright © Brandon Chao-Chi Yen, 2016

First published in English by Balestier Press in 2016

ISBN 978 0 9932154 7 6

This book was published with the support
of the National Museum of Taiwan Literature.

Contents

Note on Names

Surnames precede first names in the Chinese language. In Taiwan, full names are often used, even amongst family members and close friends. A person whose first name consists of only one Chinese character is almost always addressed by the full name, as in the case of Lin Bin. First names with two Chinese characters are hyphenated. These practices are preserved throughout the translation. The following is a list of the names of the seven children, their nicknames, and pronunciations (tones are marked above vowels).

Chen Yi-Xiong (*chén yì syóng*), the narrator, nickname **Glasses**
Lin Bin (*lín bin*), nickname **A-Bin** (*ah bin*) (Nicknames in the form of 'A-' are common in Taiwan.)
Wu Chun-Hua (*wú chun huá*)
Lin Wang-Xi (*lín wǎng sî*), nickname **Touch-Me-Not**
Pan Ding-Guo (*pan dìng guó*), nickname **A-Pan** (*ah pan*)
Ye Ying-San (*yè ying san*)
Chen Xiang-Zhen (*chén siang jhen*)

1

Do you still remember the promise made twenty years ago?

The promenade deck is slightly trembling. Astern of the ship, the propeller breaks the water into splashing noises. The Taipeng ferry I'm on is about to leave Kaohsiung Port, sailing towards my hometown.

Leaning against the railings, I send my glance around: the morning sun, mellow and gentle, has just penetrated the gap between the hills; one ray after another, its light is incorporated into the sea mist rising from the stern. Within only an instant, a rainbow, shaped like an overbridge, has materialised over the port. Our ferry turns round, passing through the arch of the rainbow.

In the distance, the houses that stand upright like a forest—as well as the nearby warehouses of Kaohsiung

Port and the lighthouse on Qijin Island—are all spinning backwards. The gigantic vessels berthed in the port, hearing the reverberating sound of the steam whistle, which signifies our departure, are languidly waking up, as if, shaken by the rolling waves, they were stretching and yawning—all of them still half buried in their slumbers.

I gaze upon the port, which is vanishing little by little into the distance, gulp down a mouthful of sea air, which has a fishy, salty odour, and cannot help but burst into laughter!

Twenty years ago, when I left Penghu's Magong Port, standing upon the deck and casting one last glance at my hometown, did I not have the same feeling? It was this subtle dizziness, these waves of thought coming and going, while everything before me was retreating into all directions. It was the land that was moving and trembling; it was my hometown that was gradually leaving me behind. Not until the ferry had sailed beyond the bounds of the harbour—the steam whistle once again sent forth its resonating peal, the land had disappeared, and the waves were raging against the hull—did it dawn upon me, with a sudden shudder in my heart, that it was I who was leaving it all behind.

After all these years, I have decided to return to my hometown in the same way because, as I once left it sea mile by sea mile—leaving behind that archipelago composed of sixty-four isles—so I want to approach it again sea mile by sea mile now: the isles of Hujing, Bazhao, Hua, Tongpan… I want them to watch me serenely from outside Magong Port—watch me, always a son of Penghu, come back to my hometown.

An aeroplane moves too fast. They wouldn't be able to see me clearly. The comfort on the plane couldn't allay my nervousness. Only the sea wind that blows against the hull can dry my sweating palms; it alone can give those isles, bit by bit, a full view of me.

That promise made twenty years ago—how many people will remember it?

Time has left its mark on everyone. We're all grown up, mature, some of us gaining weight, others becoming thinner. Even if our facial features and expressions look the same, can it be possible that we still think the same way? Will the friendship that once bound us together, leavened by time, turn out to be attenuated, or all the stronger?

Twenty years—in retrospect, it seems just a transient moment. But when I look more closely, time lays itself out before me, like an interminable road winding its way through a rough terrain interspersed with myriads of mountains and rivers. No one can ever thread them all together. With a bitter smile, I shake my head, asking myself this question:

So I'm back. This very date has never escaped my memory; will others remember it too? Ye Ying-San and Chen Xiang-Zhen should remember it well.

What about the Thin Boy, Lin Bin?

Might A-Pan and Touch-Me-Not have forgotten about it?

And Wu Chun-Hua?

Have we all been well, the seven of us, since we parted? Those precious ties nourished by sweat and tears—might it be possible that they will have been withered by relentless time? What will it feel like when we meet again? These questions are enmeshed in more bewildering questions.

We've all entered middle age, and Brother-in-Law is well beyond middle age.

It was he who proposed this promise, with his own clear, sonorous voice. 'Twenty years from today, on the night of the Mid-Autumn Festival, when the moon sits high in the sky above Fort Xitai, please come back here for a reunion,' he said. 'And for each of you who makes it back, I will prepare a present. Until then, please take good care of yourselves.'

We, being young, were excitedly making guesses at what presents Brother-in-Law would bring us. He smiled but said nothing, leaving us to our wild guesses. A while later he added: 'There will be no reason for being shy. Some of you will have had a splendid career. Perhaps others will still be groping. It doesn't matter. Do come back if you can remember. This pottery workshop will never be closed to you. If you come, you can always enter. Bear this in mind!'

The melody of the waves is wafted to my ears. I feel as if I had set foot upon that beach again.

Our pottery lessons were drawing to a close. The bonfire, lit for the farewell party, was blazing heartily. We stood, sat, and walked, our laughter bouncing here and there around the bonfire. No one seemed to understand what it meant to say good-bye.

Brother-in-Law, short and stalwart, was standing upon a block of coral stone.

Behind him stood a windbreak of horsetail trees

and densely populated white popinacs, which grew in abundance in our hometown.

The lemon-yellow moon and the flickering bonfire shone upon his face. The scar above the tip of his eyebrow was faintly visible. The spirited and earnest look on his face made me wonder whether I would ever come across such a good teacher again, a teacher who would guide me on the way to knowledge. I wondered whether Chun-Hua and the others, like me, felt sorry for Sister.

'I for one will remember,' Ye Ying-San was the first to speak. And loudly he spoke: 'And if we meet during these twenty years, no one should mention this again. We'll see who forgets about it in the end.'

Chun-Hua and Touch-Me-Not made their way to the big cauldron over the bonfire to scoop up the peanuts, which were then carried to us, steaming hot. Chun-Hua peeled some of the peanuts for me, asking: 'We cooked these peanuts for your farewell party. Will you remember today's promise?'

Lin Bin answered on my behalf, before anyone else could say anything: 'Of course Glasses will remember it. He values our friendship most. And he likes presents too!'

Gales of laughter, billowing across the bonfire, flung themselves upon me. To my surprise, those rows of horsetail trees, glistening in the fiery light and trembling in the sea breeze, seemed at this moment to join the uproar, laughing so hard as to appear to bend over.

A-Pan suddenly rose, turned his face to the moon, and began to sing that famous song he had adapted, 'The Sea Sheds Water'.

In the meanwhile, the moon was hanging high above Fort Xitai on Fisherman's Isle, illuminating our tranquil Penghu Bay. The isles, shaped like straight-mouthed clay pots around the bay, were also set aglow by the moon above the sea.

A-Pan sang and sang. Sad at heart, I picked up a twig and poked the embers of the bonfire. Then, along the wildly soaring sparks, I sent my eyes abroad to the night sky, which resembled an ink-blue vault made of glass, also glittering above our heads.

Does everyone still remember? Are all my old friends well, after all these years?

So solemn was the promise that Brother-in-Law made that night. What on earth will be the presents he is preparing for us?

* * *

The ferry is thrown into jolting convulsions. I hold fast onto the railings, looking around, flustered. A spatter of water crashes down upon the deck without any warning, making half of my clothes wet. Around the hull is a foaming hem churning and bouncing on all sides. Everything suddenly blurs in my eyes. Gripped by a nauseating dizziness, I can only sense that the ferry is moving upwards and downwards.

An old man with a swarthy complexion grasps my arm, saying: 'Don't stand here, young man. Go into the cabins for a rest. You visitors don't know the danger. People get swept into this Black Water Trough.'

There are a few fixed iron benches inside the ferry. We seat ourselves.

'You don't know. The sea is deepest here, the wind and waves most ferocious. Two ocean currents converge here. But it'll be alright in a quarter of an hour or so. Do you get seasick? From your looks, I can tell at once that you're coming to Penghu on holiday!'

'Sir, I'm also from Penghu. I've just come back from Canada.'

'Oh young man, you're joking, aren't you?' Intense scrutiny follows. He splays my hand out and presses my palm. 'Are you sure? Your palm is soft and delicate. You're wearing glasses. Such a gentle look… And you say you're from Penghu? Are you sure?' The old man taps on the bench back, gesturing towards an isle on the right, saying: 'But you can't fool me. Let me ask you. What's the name of that island?'

The vessel having sailed across the Black Water Trough, the view over the sea has cleared up. Just a single glance, and I know exactly what lies ahead of me. 'The one in front is General's Isle. Behind it is Bazhao Isle.'

A flock of seabirds flit across the lighthouse on Fisherman's Isle and progress towards the vessel in a light, elegant movement. 'What are these birds? Any ideas?' the old man asks again.

I adjust my glasses, looking up. 'Bridled terns! They live on Mao Isle.'

'Brilliant! You have the right answers! Absolutely brilliant!' The old man claps his hands and laughs. 'If only all youngsters in Penghu were like you. Are you coming back for the Mid-Autumn Festival?'

Hearing the old man's coarse voice and hearty laughter, and seeing the isles, lighthouse, and seabirds that are welcoming me, I know I'm back.

Although everyone in my family has left Penghu, this gradual approach stirs up such feelings as make me answer the old man without any hesitation: 'Yes, I am. I am coming home.'

2

What 'fruit wish' did you make?

Magong Port has put on a new face.

An imposing twelve-story mansion stands in the noontide sun. The tiles on the roof of Tianhou Temple have been refurbished. Fashionably dressed people are weaving their ways in front of the lofty building of the port terminal. Had it not been for a sign on the pier saying 'Welcome to Penghu', I could never have believed that the ferry had brought me to Magong Port.

A squat, middle-aged man rushes out of the port terminal and stands still on the wharf, resting a palm on his forehead while he looks out towards the vessel. Such a familiar gesture!

At the prow, a sailor swings the loop and flings it onto the wharf. 'Will you help me haul it up?' he shouts.

The squat, middle-aged man hurries to pick up the loop, hauls by the hawser, and ties it around a bollard on the wharf. In the meanwhile, he raises his head twice or three times, looking searchingly towards the crowds emerging from the boarding gangway. Something in his eyes stirs my memory. Was he a childhood neighbour? Or did we study in neighbouring classes perhaps?

With a basket of Irwin mangoes in one hand, I'm walking at the back of the queue, feeling a tug at my heartstrings, but there's a slight weakness in my limbs. Ah! I'm about to step onto my homeland!

The squat, middle-aged man sees me, jumps high in the air, and darts away on the wharf, waving at me desperately as he makes his way towards the gangway to get on board. But the passengers are descending from the vessel; unable to squeeze himself through, he runs towards the bollard, clambers up, and waves from there. It is only at this moment that I spot a six or seven-year-old boy beside him, who pulls at his trousers, yelling anxiously: 'Daddy, it's too dangerous!'

Hearing this, the man scoops the little boy up onto the bollard and tells him to wave at me as well.

'Chen Yi-Xiong! Glasses!'

He shouts my name, in a voice loud enough for everyone in Magong to hear very clearly. I don't know how to answer him. In a fluster, the wicker basket that contains the Irwin mangoes gets caught on the railings along the boarding gangway. I cannot proceed; nor can I turn round. Meanwhile, the squat, middle-aged man, pulling his boy along, has already dashed to the bottom of the gangway. He snatches my mangoes and lands a fist on me, which makes me stumble backwards. 'Glasses! I was right. I knew you would remember it. I knew you would come back today by ship. I'm here to welcome you, with my boy.' He finds me bewildered and gives me another strike on the shoulder. 'You don't recognise me?' With arms akimbo, he looks even bigger, even more corpulent. 'I'm the Thin Boy, Lin Bin, A-Bin—' he yells.

Can it be Lin Bin? So completely out of shape! It's almost like a different person, infinitely growing sideways, like a shrunken balloon being blown larger and larger! We look each other up and down, take a step back for a clearer scrutiny, and burst into laughter, wild laughter. I laugh so hard that I have to hold my glasses quickly. We have a fierce hug, as if we were in a wrestling match, as if we wanted to crush each other's bones with a single embrace.

'Don't you laugh at me! The more I work, the fatter I get. Now you see this "lifebuoy" on my waist. There's no helping it.' Lin Bin lifts his son up in his arms, telling him to call me 'Uncle'. Upon inspection, the boy indeed appears to be a small version of Lin Bin in his teens—a little nose, big eyes, dark and shimmering skin, not at all timid no matter whom he sees. He looks at the mangoes in the basket, saying: 'Your mangoes are not delicious!'

'How did you know?'

'You didn't give me any.' He wrinkles his nose, looking over his shoulder to ask his dad: 'Am I right?'

'Yes, Little Bao. You've got to be careful, though. He was our Class Leader. If you don't behave well, he'll record it.' Lin Bin presses his son closer to himself and laughs.

'Glasses, you have a good memory. You did bring these mangoes. Don't tell me. Let's see if I can remember what fruit wish each of us made at the farewell party twenty years ago. The Irwin mango was what Brother-in-Law and Wu Chun-Hua wanted. Touch-Me-Not wanted to imitate Yang Guifei* and eat three hundred lychees in one go. A-Pan said even in his dreams he was eating wax apples. And I? What wish did I make?'

'Who knows!' I join the laughter of father and son.

'Now I'm the most senior driver working for Penghu's public bus services. You didn't know we also had bus services here in Penghu, did you?' Lin Bin asks. 'Today I changed my shift to two o'clock, just to pick you up, to drive you to Brother-in-Law's pottery workshop. The passengers will come and go, but do think of it as a bus specially reserved for you.' He laughs again, his face reddening with laughter, and his flesh quivering restlessly.

'Has everyone else arrived?'

'Not a clue. There's still plenty of time before "the moon sits high in the sky above Fort Xitai". It is, I'm afraid, not very probable that everyone will show up.'

'Do you see them often?'

'Surely not!' Lin Bin leads me towards the main street, along which is a ribbon of art and craft shops, photography shops, and barbershops, whose windows are resplendently decorated. It's as if I were walking into the streets of Taipei City. 'I saw Wang-Xi getting her groceries in the market

---

* Yang Guifei (719-756) was a beloved concubine of Emperor Xuanzong of the Tang Dynasty.

this morning,' Lin Bin says. 'She's running a cafeteria. She's a boss now. Two years ago A-Pan was singing on the television. He came back once for the New Year holidays. But I haven't heard from him recently.'

'What about Brother-in-Law? Yin-San and the others?'

'Don't get anxious! Those who should come will come. We'll know when we meet, won't we?'

'Did you remind Wang-Xi that we're going to meet this evening?'

'Surely a person who really cares doesn't need such nagging! I deliberately kept silent, just to test her! This busy woman, revolving like a whirlwind in the market square… I think she has probably forgotten about it.'

Lin Bin is indeed out of shape, but he still has the same old temperament. He takes me to the dome-like bus station. It's two o'clock sharp, his shift time. The three veiled women in the station, seeing us walk in, exclaim: 'Here you are, Lin Bin! We thought you were too dead-drunk again to mind your duty.'

Lin Bin shakes his head, smiling bitterly. 'Why are you embarrassing me like this? It was one of the rarest occasions, and you've been teasing me for years.' He asks me: 'Do you know who they are? Cui-Hua, Yan-Jin, and Mei-Ling, the Three Flowers in our neighbouring class. They get on my bus everyday to go and pluck sea-lavenders and to make coral necklaces. On the bus, I've made it a habit not to pay them the least attention—to avoid troubles.'

Lin Bin's son tells me seriously: 'My dad has quit drinking. My mum doesn't allow him. Those aunties are lying.'

Lin Bin joyously hoists his son into the bus, exhorting him thus: 'Say only the first half. The second half is not so necessary.'

I can't help laughing. 'Drop me off in front of the school.'

'Aren't you heading for Brother-in-Law's place?'

'I'll go there after dark. I'd like to have a walk in our school first. Is that vast field of gaillardias still there in front of the school entrance?'

'Gaillardias? Ah…' Lin Bin taps on the steering wheel, and the bus begins to move. 'They're blooming all over the place. They always attract my attention too whenever I drive past. Yes, perhaps you should get off there,' he says.

3

I am that bad boy!

Such a hillside, which everywhere regales the eye with a rich profusion of yellow flowers, I have seen elsewhere, a few times. That immense field of tulips in Amsterdam and that prairie carpeted with penstemon flowers in Latin America—both of them were more voluptuous and expansive compared with this bed of gaillardias. But this hillside of gaillardias remembers the footsteps of my youthful days. The flowers here shared my laughter while I was growing up. Treasured deep inside the soil are our tears. Is there any place that bears comparison? For me, this is the most beautiful flowerbed of them all.

Getting off the bus in front of the school, I squat down and gaze upon the hillside, the one which I have seen so many times in my dreams.

People in my hometown are used to squatting when they chat, squatting when they eat, and squatting when they do business. Whenever we visited this hillside of gaillardias, we too made it a habit to squat down and watch the flowers toss their heads in the blustery sea wind. People say gaillardias have no smell, but we were able to detect the special odour given off by these tens of thousands of them. Stir wisps of tea fragrance into some smoke of burning hay and into the slightly fishy tang of sea air—blend all of these together—and you get the scent of gaillardias.

The gaillardias are still here. I'm like a lost wayfarer who, after a long journey, finally comes across a signpost he wishes to follow, which gives him peace of mind.

Even more to my surprise, three or four cows are grazing leisurely on the hillside, slowly pacing around and stretching their necks to search amongst the grass for food, with their long-haired tails swinging here and there. The background shows a fringe of flat-topped isles and the serene sea—exactly as it was twenty years ago. For a second, I can't tell whether the scene before me is a replica, or whether I have returned to those youthful days.

* * *

That year, we were fifteen-year-old boys and girls.

On the afternoon following the day the US's Surveyor 3 landed on the Moon, Lin Bin and I were driven out of the classroom by our Geography teacher.

My satchel was still in the classroom. Standing outside

the windows, I heard the Geography teacher fiercely scolding the class: 'What kind of class am I teaching! With such a Class Leader! Insulting your teacher in such a brazen manner. I've lost all hope in you!'

Before long, Lin Bin came out too, swinging two satchels.

We walked ahead without looking back, all the while kicking at knobs of earth, saying nothing, and making our way straight out of the school entrance.

I couldn't bear the mocking tone of our Geography teacher any longer. He had said this more than once: 'I've never drunk any well water that was not sweet, except for that in Penghu, which is salty. You don't need to put any salt when you cook. Cook luffa gourds, and it will turn out like a bitter melon soup, because the water here also has a bitter taste.' While saying this, he broke into convulsive laughter despite us. 'And your wind robs people of banknotes! I went out into the streets the other day, checked every shop, but couldn't find any tasty food anywhere. People were selling dried fish everywhere. What? Did they expect me to carry dried fish back to my room and eat it with your salty water? I settled for a bag of peanuts. And guess what? The moment I pulled my banknotes out of my pocket, the northeast monsoon, which you are so proud of, robbed me of everything. What kind of place is this! Annoying, isn't it? You can't even enjoy your peanuts.'

The class cackled with him. 'You probably haven't watched any African films,' he continued. 'That kind of place, where people are scorched by day and frozen by night—despite this, loads of people still live there. Stupid!

Like me. Why didn't I stay in good old Taiwan? Why did I come to Penghu to suffer? Don't laugh. You're not better than me.' The more he talked, the more enthusiastic he became, and he began to hit his own palm with his pointer. 'Rightly goes the old saying: "When heaven intends to confer a great office on a man, it will first frustrate his mind, exhaust his sinews, expose his body to starvation, and subjugate his life to indigence." Henceforth, probably we'll all become great people!'

Once again, my classmates pounded their desks and laughed with the Geography teacher. This was beyond my endurance. I stood up and shouted: 'What are you laughing at?' The class looked at me, shamefacedly. Our Geography teacher was stunned too. He leant his back against the blackboard, observing me with his head tilted. The jolly creases around his mouth were smoothed out little by little.

'Sir, is there no gale in your hometown? Is there no thunder?'

'Why are you asking this?'

I could hear the rat-a-tat of my heart, which was beating like a rattle drum.

Recalling his words—'everyone in Penghu reeks of a fishy odour, as a result of which, flocks of cats follow them while they're walking'—I couldn't help but tremble with anger; stammering and faltering, I could only yell these words at him: 'Did you come from paradise?'

The class burst into restrained laughter. I banged my desk, exclaiming: 'Don't you laugh!'

'Banging your desk? Is this what your teachers have

taught you? And you're the Class Leader!' The Geography teacher waxed furious. He walked down from the podium and said: 'I'll tell you. In my hometown, every season is agreeable. We've got rice, fruit, and everything, everything you can imagine.'

'But why are you still staying in Penghu, Sir?' Lin Bin asked.

For a moment, our Geography teacher was at a loss for words. After a while, he replied: 'Are you allowed to ask this? I'm teaching Geography. Everything I say is based on facts. Stand up, Lin Bin.'

'You're criticising Penghu, Sir, as if there were nothing worth bothering with here.'

The entire class sizzled with whispers. Having heard these words, no one dared give free reign to laughter any more.

'Did I mean this? Chen Yi-Xiong!'

I stared at the teacher, not intending to give any answer.

'Very well. If you don't want to listen, then don't come to my class. Get out! Both of you. Get out!'

Lin Bin and I crossed the road and found ourselves on the hillside ablaze with gaillardias.

We squatted down, saw three or four cows ambling on the hillside, and watched the gaillardias tossing their heads in the northeast monsoon, which still lingered in early spring. My heart resembled a white cloud suspended in the blue sky. The blue sky was so spacious, but the cloud suspended there seemed somewhat nervous.

All the taunts of our Geography teacher paled in comparison with that final sentence of his: 'Everything I say is based on facts.' I had to admit that:

Our water was salty. And it did have a bitter taste.

Our soil was barren. True, no crop would grow in abundance here.

The northeast monsoon lasted half a year. Even the rampart-like horsetail trees and coral stones could not keep it at bay!

Our bodies smelled of fish. Indeed, who of us—islanders who lived off the sea—could avoid partaking of its smell? Even our hair and our fingertips reeked of that fresh, raw odour of dried fish.

Like a matador who, being deprived of his cape and sword, suddenly finds himself fighting empty-handed in the full glare of the spectators, I felt as if my heart were lifted up to mid-air by sadness and embarrassment. It couldn't rise upwards; nor was there any way down. I could only squat disconsolately and hate Penghu!

Unable to think myself out of this, I fondled the gaillardias with my fingers, nonchalantly trying to pluck one. I pinched its stalk with two fingers but couldn't pluck it off. Then, clenching it with my entire hand, I exerted more force, but the flower was still tenaciously clinging to the barren yellow soil. My heart shuddered, and my eyes grew sharp.

Lin Bin moved closer, looked carefully, and extended a hand to help me, as though we were trying to pull up a turnip. Then we pulled, using so much force that the entire flower was uprooted. Its primary root was broken, buried deep inside the soil, but its thin fibrous roots clutched with them a handful of yellow soil! We fell onto the ground on our backs. Surprisingly, both of us laughed.

The whole gaillardia was in my hand. My head and my face were spattered with bits of yellow soil.

'It's strange that this kind of flower, small as it is, should have such a deep root.'

Gaillardias were rampant in Penghu, growing densely; beyond the peanut fields, beside the graveyards, they could be seen everywhere. I had grown used to them since childhood. Low and unassuming, they were just like the sea surrounding us in all directions—how many Penghu people would cast a second look? We simply took them for granted. We thought they had always been there, everywhere.

A-Bin continued to lead the way until we reached the cows. Each of us chose a cow, mounted, and sat astride it. We hung the gaillardia on a horn. The cows tamely yielded to us, treading their paths hither and thither on the flowery hillside.

'Is your dad still talking about moving?' Lin Bin asked.

The bristles on the cow's back scratched my calves—not so much prickly as tickly. I patted the cow on the back gently and nodded.

'Will you go to another school?' Lin Bin asked again.

'My dad has opened a coral business in Taipei. He moved there first. When everything is settled, we'll follow him.'

'Oh, it seems that people are daily moving out of Penghu. One day, this place will be deserted, and the empty houses will all become birdhouses—a Paradise for Birds.' Lin Bin drew circles with a finger on the back of his cow, directing his glance across the deep blue sea in Penghu Bay. His thin and small body rose and fell to the rhythms of the cow's paces. 'To be honest,' he said, 'our Geography teacher wasn't blabbering. If one had a choice, who would stay in this place, where "not a bird wants to lay its eggs"? If even we Penghu people are moving out, can we expect others to stay? Those who remain are people like my family. We can't move. We can only stay here and drink salty water, bear the northeast monsoon.'

When Lin Bin was in his sixth year of primary school, his father, a drunkard, tumbled from a boat and was never seen again. His mother went to the seaside everyday to pick crowned turban shells, to collect little seashells to thread them into necklaces, and to gather seaweed when the tide was low in Penghu Bay. It was thanks to our teacher, who had pleaded for him, that Lin Bin was allowed to attend junior high school. I was worried for him. If his mother had known that he was driven out of the classroom by a teacher, what a rage she would have flown into! I asked Lin Bin. He shook his head, saying: 'I don't know, and you?'

'Mum would want me to apologise.' I leapt down from the cow's back, flinging my head around. 'Out of the question! Even if all he said was true, he shouldn't have said it that way. He despises Penghu,' I said.

The class bell tolled. Lin Bin and I looked over our shoulders. Before long, a few people ran out of the school entrance, peering in all directions. Lin Bin said: 'Wu Chun-Hua, Touch-Me-Not, A-Pan, and Sister! They brought Sister here.'

A-Pan called out to us, but as soon as he made his voice

heard, Chun-Hua gripped him. The four of them ran towards the hillside of gaillardias. Sister said something to them, upon which the group suddenly formed themselves into a single queue, making their way slowly.

A-Bin and I leant against a cow, lowering our heads to gaze on the gaillardias, which were all over the place. They arrived, A-Pan, Chun-Hua, and Wang-Xi standing behind Sister. Seeing that we were silent, Sister said: 'Flower viewing?'

A-Bin and I couldn't have heard it wrong. Flower viewing? We? We couldn't help but break into laughter.

'While everyone was being scolded in the classroom, you came out here to ride cows, view flowers, watch the sea, and relax. You certainly know how to enjoy life.' Sister tilted her face and stared at A-Bin and me, studying us earnestly.

Hearing what Sister said, A-Pan and the others couldn't hold back either; together, we laughed uproariously—laughed until we couldn't breathe and began to cough, until I felt like crying.

Sister was our homeroom teacher. She had been teaching at our school for only two years. I dare say she was the teacher most beloved of the whole class.

Except that she was much given to tears, everything about her was perfect. We all loved to read her 'Homeroom Teacher's Comments' in our weekly journals. Who knew us better than Sister?

In the previous semester's inter-class football matches, we had beaten the title-holder Class 3-A. We were so happy that we wept on each other's shoulders. Sister's cotton shirt was smeared, like a tablecloth, with our sweat and tears. She led the girls to serve drinks to all the 'football heroes'. We all seated ourselves between the goalposts. She took the lead and exclaimed: 'Bottoms up!'

'Thanks to Madam's effective leadership, we demonstrated such prowess, such solidarity really,' Lin Bin delivered his speech in a very formal manner, totally self-possessed.

The girls, whose voices had broken because of their loud cheers, mumbled in tears: 'Madam, please don't leave us. You're our most beloved teacher.'

'Who said I was leaving you?' Sister blushed and gathered up her hair, which was blown wild by the sea wind. Smilingly, she said: 'You're all my little brothers and sisters. I'm your elder sister. We're a family. Who said I was leaving?'

From that time on, we all called her Sister, but only behind her back.

* * *

News travelled fast. A-Bin's and my expulsion from the classroom caused a sensation in the school within just an hour.

After school that day, on my way home, I was aware that all the students who took the same route were watching me. I feigned innocence, ignoring them but still walking faster and faster. Not until I was stopped by a tall figure did I realise I had left the group of students far behind.

'I heard you had taught the Geography teacher a lesson?

You don't look like it—I underestimated you.' The person in front of me stood with his legs wide apart, shaking them. 'He said the same thing several times in our class too,' he continued. 'I wanted to correct him, but I dared not. You gave vent to my anger. Come, shall we shake hands? You don't know me?' He spoke in a flat voice, as if he were clenching a toothpick between his teeth.

Not in the right mood to answer him, I resumed my strides. But that person persevered and chased.

'Surely a Class Leader is also a human being? A shake won't make your hands dirty, won't turn you into a bad person. Don't you worry!' He stuck out his hand. His legs, wider apart now, decisively blocked my progress. 'You really don't know me? I'm the one whom those cowards call "that bad boy" behind my back.'

This rang a bell. The boy was called Ye Ying-San, and this was confirmed by a glance at the name-tag on his shirt. In the run-up to the Model Student Election in the previous semester, he had taken part in the campaign for the candidate nominated by our neighbouring class. He had positioned himself on a wooden fish crate set up by himself, resting one hand on his waist and making a fist with the other. Every single speech of his was heavily attended. After I had lost the election, Wu Chun-Hua and Lin Bin hated him to the core, complaining that he had swayed all the voters to his side.

'Your homeroom teacher went to the hillside to find you. I saw it. What did she tell you? I want to know,' Ye Ying-San said. 'I've heard she's a nice person. I want to know how she deals with this.'

'Aren't you poking your nose in too far?' I bypassed him and walked in big strides. 'She said, such a vast field of gaillardias is nowhere to be seen, except here in Penghu. Although the soil is dry, water scarce, and the wind so strong, the flowers are still in full bloom. Tomorrow morning, she'll go with us and talk to the Geography teacher.'

'What?' He looked at me with a blank confusion, apparently not having understood my words. 'And then? Did she say she would record it as a Major Demerit? Could it possibly have ended like this?'

'It doesn't give you enough of a buzz?'

'Huh! For real! This Class Leader is formidable. If I had been you, I would have run for my life!' Ye Ying-San blew air through his nostrils, saying: 'Your homeroom teacher is a real legend. No wonder our Arts and Crafts teacher loves her so much.'

'Who?'

'You're the Class Leader, and you don't know this? Every time he sees your teacher, his eyes discharge electricity. Electricity!' Ye Ying-San's claw-like fingers danced wildly in front of his eyes. He added: 'But he can't do it properly. Now it's on, now off. I think he's also a coward. I'm talking about Tao Pei-Jia. He seems to have some character. If your teacher ever felt the electricity, she should count herself lucky.'

Mr Tao was our Arts and Crafts teacher too. Why didn't we know this?

'You're really paying attention to everyone at school, aren't you? You want to discover who it is that you have offended, who does what to whom, and who says you're a bad boy. Am I right?'

'You four-eyed swot, you are brave. No one has dared say that to me. You're the first, ever.' Ye Ying-San clenched his jaw and smiled, lifting his face to the sky, and smashing a nugget of soil with the tip of a foot. 'I was right about you, then. In the football matches, you were terrible, but your courage impressed me. What you did today lived up to my impression. You're the man. I want us to be friends.'

'We're schoolmates already.'

'That's different,' he said, quite seriously. 'I don't want to call you Class Leader. I'm not given to flattery. I've no time for those boring titles. I want to call you Glasses.'

Meanwhile I was pondering over the rumour of Mr Tao wooing our Sister.

This was all very marvellous. I was worried and happy at the same time. Mr Tao was full of fresh ideas. A bunch of needle-shaped horsetail tree leaves, a clump of sand, and some seashells, once fallen into his hands, would soon be turned into beautiful artworks.

Ye Ying-San said he had 'some character'. Did this refer to his reticence, his characteristic gaze upon a window, a tree, a cow—indeed, upon everything?

When I came to think about it, Mr Tao was in fact rather popular amongst us too.

He was not tall. You could even say he was a bit short. The girls all said he was one of those exquisite little fellows. Oh yes! He liked to wear cotton shirts. This matched our Sister. Surely he wasn't in thrall to her?

He also loved to wear black kung-fu shoes. It looked

slightly odd, but it didn't put us off as much as his untidy hair. Why didn't he comb it properly? Perhaps Ye Ying-San's 'some character' epithet sprang from his admiration for Mr Tao's bristly, bedraggled hair?

'Mr Tao goes to the hillside quite often these days, to dig and play with clay. He's building a big stove, to bake stuff like bottles and teapots. He invited me over the other day, wanting to teach me. Hey, why me, me alone?' Ye Ying-San continued: 'Glasses, I'm a bad student. Being my friend is dangerous. I'll give you three days to consider it.'

That was our first confrontation. We walked a long distance together along a muddy road. Perhaps that bizarre kind of conversation—one spiced with gunpowder but with a yearning for friendship too—only occurs between youths who are both proud and diffident?

Such a person—twenty years on, what would have become of him?

4

Please come to the pottery workshop

I pluck off a gaillardia, stick it into the wattled basket of Irwin mangoes, and set off towards the school entrance. Like a child going to school for the first time, I feel excited, but even more than this excitement, there's a sense of apprehension.

I know very well that they have a day-off for the Mid-Autumn Festival: the campus is empty; only a few Formosan dogs are walking about. Despite this, I find myself pacing warily, fearing that the next step, which will bring me round the corridor's corner, might suddenly reveal my youthful self, as if I would bump straight into an apparition of what I was, a ghost from twenty years ago.

The dogs accompany me on my inspection of one classroom after another.

There are three rows of classrooms, no more or less than there used to be. They don't seem to have aged either, only that the sharp lines along the edges of the roofs have been smoothed over by sandy wind, and the square columns in the corridors have been rounded off. Coming to what used to be our classroom, I stick my face close to the windowpanes to look inside. The new blackboard is mostly wiped clean. But on one side of it are written the virtues of the week—industry and frugality—and the names of the students on duty—Chen Jin-Tong and Lin Man-Zai (Big-Head Zai).

'Big-Head Zai'—can it be that there are two people in this class sharing the same name Lin Man-Zai, so they need the differentiating epithet? Laughter ensues. The names of the students on duty can't be erased. They have to be especially clear. If not, there would be a row the next morning.

What does the youth look like who has my old seat beside the window? Perhaps he also wears glasses; hence his choice of the most well-lit place by the window. This window could never be thoroughly closed. Sands sifted in through the chink. One could never finish wiping them off. Perhaps he also has this trouble.

The horsetail trees outside the windows, over the past twenty years, have neither aged nor grown. The side of them facing northeast is bald. The treetops, reminiscent of youths with flattops, are neatly shaven by the wind, their growths cut short at the level of the eaves.

During one of our scouting lessons, we had a campfire feast under these horsetail trees.

Chun-Hua and Wang-Xi were our chefs. Boys were dispatched to fetch water and gather twigs. We all fell to our tasks boisterously.

Chun-Hua, like Sister, was from Wu Village. In Penghu, girls from Wu Village were famously capable. It was a village where men were in charge of domestic work, while women busied themselves with outdoor tasks. Tillage and cultivation in the fields were carried out by those veiled women. Girls there did not marry out of the village; they kept to a matrilocal tradition. Chun-Hua was not veiled, but she was a very capable girl: washing and cutting vegetables, sautéing spices and stir-frying rice vermicelli—her movements were so nimble that our eyes could hardly catch up. With one hand on her waist and the other reaching out for a taste, she looked exactly like a chef. She was the Chief of Service in our class. Even Lin Bin had to bow down to her commands; no slovenly behaviour was to be tolerated!

Wang-Xi, on the contrary, was an introverted person. She didn't talk much, only quietly performing her duties. We all said she was more timid than sparrows hiding in horsetail trees. When we talked to her, we had to lower our voices. If not, she would be frightened into tears. She was always biting her nails, her eyes lowered, not daring to look people in the eyes. And her right shoulder was, more often than not, slightly raised, with the ends of her hair hanging over it. It was as if she were constantly on guard against someone who might hit her. We called her Touch-Me-Not: not to be touched. But very strangely, once she was committed to a task, no one, except for Chun-Hua, could ever compare with her.

With the aluminium lids of our lunch boxes in our hands, we seated ourselves next to one another, eating stir-fried rice vermicelli under the horsetail trees outside the windows. In the midst of our casual conversations, I revealed to the class the story of Mr Tao taking a fancy to Sister.

Everyone halted; their mouths were stuffed with rice vermicelli, as if, having burned their tongues, they were keeping their mouths open, waiting for the heat to go.

'Wait, let me think…' Chun-Hua rose to her feet, hushing everyone. 'It's true! So it was Mr Tao. I've seen it twice. So it was him. Both incidents happened after dark. It was unbearably cold. Those dogs at the entrance to our village were barking so hard…'

'Why, it's like a horror film.' A-Pan jostled forward, making us tickle all over and chuckle without stopping.

'A human shape was swaying about here and there at the village entrance, with a torch flashing on and off. Whoever it was was there for around three minutes. I saw this very clearly; it was Sister who went out. Same on both occasions. Less than one minute, and Sister turned her head and walked back.'

'So quick! How can a date end so quickly?' Lin Bin asked.

'I was wondering too. Like a batter being struck out during a baseball game, the man lingered on at our village entrance in a vacant mood for a while before he left. In such a cold weather, he came with a torch to see someone, only to be struck out. At that time, I took so much pity on him that I could barely focus on my homework again. But it's astonishing that the man should have been Mr Tao.'

'He could have sought her out at school. Why did he go there after dark? He's so strange.'

'A-Pan, be quiet if you don't know. There are so many people here in our school. How could they have let out their feelings here?' Chun-Hua continued. 'Mr Tao must be too shy. We should encourage him to persevere. He's a very nice person. If he marries Sister, he'll become our brother-in-law.'

It was during the campfire feast that day that we began to call Mr Tao Brother-in-Law.

On the afternoon of the same day, the loudspeakers belched out seven names in a continuous stream. I was the first, followed by Wu Chun-Hua, Lin Bin, Lin Wang-Xi, Pan Ding-Guo, Ye Ying-San, and Chen Xiang-Zhen. The person who made the announcement was none other than our Brother-in-Law, Mr Tao.

'So soon!' Chun-Hua was astounded. 'Who let on the secret? Who's got such a big mouth as to report such a thing to him?' she yelled.

Ye Ying-San and Chen Xiang-Zhen ran to us from the neighbouring class, aghast. 'I'm not one of your gang, Glasses. Who dragged me into this? You bunch of oh-so-good students, don't pretend you're innocent and then stab people in the back.'

For Lin Bin and me, perhaps it was because of our having been driven out of the classroom. But why A-Pan and Touch-Me-Not? If it had been about bringing him and Sister together, it would have been enough to summon Wu

Chun-Hua and Ye Yin-San, who first divulged the secret. Why Lin Bin and Chen Xiang-Zhen?

Vociferous and full of mutterings, the party made its way towards the Office of Student Affairs, halting at the entrance.

Brother-in-Law had been waiting for us there. Without a word, he waved at us and guided us through the playing field, along the walls, and past the incinerator, until we reached the small side entrance. The seven of us walked so close that we constantly treaded on each other's heels, bumbling along. But no one dared speak.

With both hands in the pockets of his trousers, Brother-in-Law stood in the middle of the side entrance. He tilted his heels up and down. His coarse, black hair grew wilfully wild on his head. But under his forehead, that pair of eyes faintly betrayed a smile. 'Why are you all so nervous?' he asked.

Wang-Xi was biting her nails. With his thumbs hooked under his belt, Ye Ying-San leant his back upon the wall and drooped his head, staring at all of us with his eyes hoisted. Lin Bin was cracking his knuckles, making popping noises… We resembled a gang of felons waiting to be sentenced by a judge. But the judgement was not yet pronounced—though we had walked a long distance, reaching the wall upon the yellow sand. Was it possible that we were to be executed without even being sentenced? My mind was entangled, like a fishing thread whose end was nowhere to be found; it felt unpleasant.

Brother-in-Law turned his head, looking backwards. 'Do you know where I live?' he asked.

Over his shoulder lay a hilly land. The arid, yellow ground resembled congealed waves. Rows of wind-fences, which were made of coral stone, looked exactly like breakwaters. In the distance, two flat-roofed, tiled houses, one taller, the other humbler, one bigger, the other smaller, invited comparison with sailboats dropping their anchors together. Was it one of those two houses? What about them?

'I have a pottery workshop, next to the house I live in, the bigger one there.' With his hands intertwined in front of his chest, Brother-in-Law said: 'The kiln I've been building will be finished in a couple of days. I intend to invite the seven of you to join my pottery workshop and try your hand at ceramic art. I hope everyone is interested.'

'Is that all?' Chun-Hua asked.

'Your hands are nimble, and you are creative. Although you're not the top students in your Arts and Crafts class, I can see that you have the potential.'

'Is that all?' Chun-Hua asked again.

Brother-in-Law grinned, touching his chin and staring at Chun-Hua and us. 'Why are you nervous?'

'Is there nothing else?'

'What else?'

Only then did we sigh with relief, looking at each other with daft smiles.

Once, in our Arts and Crafts class, Brother-in-Law had taught us to shape clay; but it had taken three days to sweep away all the clay fragments littering the floor afterwards. We had made ashtrays, teacups, clay figurines... those quaint, fantastic shapes never ever seen before. Sister had come to the classroom for a visit. Seeing all the clay and mud on the tables and on the floor, all that clay-dust smeared upon our hands and faces, she could only shake her head, with a bitter smile on her face.

Those 'works' were lodged by Brother-in-Law on the horizontal wood beam above the blackboard, sitting there shoulder to shoulder, as if they had been primed ready for a long exhibition. But, not having been fired in a kiln, those masterpieces of ours disappointed us: after a week, one by one, they became dry and fractured. The clay man shaped by Lin Bin announced the onset of a series of disasters, crashing into atoms during Sister's class; in the middle of our Geography class, a teacup and a work entitled 'Nameless' followed suit and crumbled to the floor. Having grasped what was going on, our teachers, whenever they were at the podium, were all put off their stroke. Finally they could bear it no more. They issued their edict, and it was the end of the exhibition.

In what sense could I be regarded as 'good' at art and craft? Lin Bin and I were birds of a feather. All things considered, only Chun-Hua and Wang-Xi could possibly merit more advanced training. What criteria had Brother-in-Law followed to select the others?

With his back against the wall, Ye Ying-San remained motionless; the corners of his eyes spelt out impatience. Finally he spoke: 'I said I didn't want to come. Why did you count me in? I've never been one for such fiddling tasks. If…'

All of a sudden, Chen Xiang-Zhen, who was in the same class as he, raised her head, striking him with two sharp rays from her eyes. Strangely, Ye Ying-San was obedient; he swallowed his words and did not continue.

'The kiln there is not completely finished. Who is there stronger than you? You can help. Would you help me build this kiln?'

Ye Ying-San did not respond. Brother-in-Law turned to ask us: 'Who has already made up their mind to join the pottery workshop?'

Silence ensued, but only for a short while. Then Chun-Hua said yes; and she nudged me! Left with no choice, I said 'I'll try'. Brother-in-Law held out his hand to me. The instant I put out mine, I felt as if I were pinched by a closing door. 'Ouch!' I shrieked, at which everybody jumped aside. 'I'm sorry. My hand is too strong,' said Brother-in-Law, embarrassed.

'What's the purpose of making pottery?' A-Pan asked.

Brother-in-Law chewed the cud for a moment and replied: 'Pottery making, from gathering, kneading, throwing, and shaping up clay to glazing, firing, and finishing a work, is a very interesting process. It promises both material and spiritual benefits.'

Moulding mud, what was there to appreciate, to gain inspiration from? Why all this abstruse philosophising! Wasn't Brother-in-Law taking it rather too seriously? I didn't understand. The same perplexity was written on the others' faces.

We Penghu people call coral stones Laogu. Laogu stones are of a light texture, quite porous. But if they're carefully stacked into walls, the northeast monsoon, however ferocious it is, when confronted with them, can only wriggle its way through, never quite knocking them down.

The footprints of the seven of us, ranged between rows of northeast-facing Laogu wind-fences, shaped themselves into a path, circuitous but distinct.

Carrying the mango basket now with the gaillardia in it, I stand at the side entrance and cast my glance abroad; that path is still there. I give my glasses one or two nudges. Can it be that the sandy wind over the last twenty years has never passed through this place? Has it been making a special effort of abstinence so that the little path can remain a memorial to our youthful days?

Those Laogu stones, which for hundreds or thousands of years have existed at the seaside, do not age, of course; it is only the unchanging pattern of the wind-fences that snags the eye.

The two flat-roofed, tiled houses, one bigger than the other, are still there at the end of the little path. Beyond them, the horsetail-tree windbreak, Penghu Bay, which is deep blue in colour, and Fort Xitai on Fisherman's Isle, above which the moon will be hanging high tonight— these have not changed either.

I stride down the stone steps at the side entrance onto the little path, yet my heart is not as agitated as I expected; what astonishes me is rather an unruffled tranquillity, as if, being away from home for a long time, I only wished to close my eyes, to ramble round the back garden, and to find out whether the soles of my feet still remember those tiny holes and those mounds of soil.

5

Make a pottery ware you like

The day Brother-in-Law's pottery workshop opened, the seven of us—surprisingly, each and every one of us—were there.

One after another, we parted company with our usual groups and met up in this new configuration at the side entrance. Chen Xiang-Zhen and Ye Ying-San took the lead; Ye Ying-San had been there already, so naturally it was he who led the way. Wang-Xi was like a timid bride, trailing at the tail of the procession; someone had to hurry her up now and then: 'Don't get lost!'

In the environs of the pottery workshop, there were no other houses in sight.

The faint footprints on the little path were probably all left by Brother-in-Law. Guided by the little path, we walked and chatted. Ye Ying-San was still repeating that trite mantra of his: 'Wanting to see me for the second time—what on earth does that mean? Asking me to mingle with you, is he not worried about me having a bad influence?'

'Did you have to go on saying that? Do you think everyone fears you, looks down on you?' Xiang-Zhen scolded him.

'I didn't want to come. It's your fault.'

'Those legs are yours. No one can force you to move.'

Despite this, Ye Ying-San was still leading the way—no hint of an intention to turn back there. Their voices were not loud, but everyone heard them. A-Pan mumbled to himself indistinctly: 'I'm worst of all at art and craft. What does Brother-in-Law want with me?'

'You don't know? Brother-in-Law's pottery workshop will also serve as a courage-training centre.' At this, we all laughed. Lin Bin continued: 'I am the one who is puzzled. You sing so well, but why is it that whenever we ask you to sing, you invariably shy away? That's why Brother-in-Law wants to give you special training.'

We all knew Lin Bin was blathering. What had pottery got to do with singing?

But in this he was telling the truth: A-Pan didn't have the nerve, and every time we asked him to sing for us, he would blush and cringe in his seat, letting down the entire class.

We marched on until we reached a place where there was a gap in a Laogu stonewall. The little path threaded its way through this gap. But a big bullock was lying prone there, secure and comfortable, blocking our progress.

'Whew! Whew! Go away!' We tried to drive it away, scare it. But Sir Bullock didn't budge an inch. It was as though someone had imagined the Laogu stonewall as the Great Wall of China and had dispatched the great beast out here to guard the gap. Seeing no hope to secure the pass through the wall, we could only make a detour round the end of the stonewall and then circle back to the little path.

We had covered a little way when we heard Wu Chun-Hua exclaim: 'Wait! Watch me!' Immediately we saw her dashing headlong. With a brisk cry, she propped her hands on the top of the Laogu stonewall and lithely leapt over it, which was as tall as a man; all her black hair was lifted, like a tern unfolding its wings—it was very beautiful indeed. We were alarmed, so much so that our impulse was to turn and run for it. But our lady had already led the bullock— by the rope attached to its nose ring—away from the gap. The little path was once again unblocked.

'Amitabha!' she said, patting herself on the breast to catch her breath. 'Problem solved. Come on. What are you looking at?' We stood dumbfounded beside the wall. Our lady walked away on her own. Longing for more, we exclaimed with one voice: 'Encore! Encore! Brava!' Chun-Hua tilted her chin, ignoring us in spite of everything.

* * *

The front door to the workshop was wide open. We took a peek, calling out softly: 'Mr Tao, Mr Tao.' There was no answer. We made a move to his house, but not a soul was to be seen there either. From outside the door, we poked our heads here and there. Set in the roof of the workshop was an enormous glass-paned skylight, like a chandelier, which rendered the interior as bright as the outside.

Hanging on the wall that fronted us were mesh screens, water ladles, and water pipes. Underneath them were potters' wheels, a workbench, and a sink.

Mounted on the sidewalls were display shelves spaced at irregular intervals.

There was another small, heavy door leading to the open air. We went round to it and found that the door opened onto an unfinished kiln. Lying there on the ground were bricks and a chimneystack. The foot of the chimneystack was stained with cement. Apparently efforts had been made to install it, but being unstable, it had been removed and was now waiting to be reinstated.

'Boys, come here,' Lin Bin suddenly shouted. 'Let's bring the chimney up!'

'You can't do it without permission. Do you know how to lay bricks?' Chun-Hua asked.

Since we had nothing else to do, we might as well perform some labour.

Under Lin Bin's command, we seriously set about stirring cement and laying bricks, installing the chimney on the roof of the kiln. Ye Ying-San's strength could rival that of any two of us combined, and he was frisky—a professional bricklayer could perhaps do no better than he.

'Seeing them messing about all the time, you wouldn't imagine they can actually do something useful.' Chun-Hua was supervising our work, talking to Chen Xiang-Zhen in the meantime. 'It's only right that these boys should do more hard labour—to make better use of their energy than creating troubles all day.' The girls nodded while talking; the more they talked, the more vehement they waxed.

There was nothing wrong in saying that Lin Bin was a joker at school. But what no one in our class knew was that Lin Bin didn't behave like that when he was at home. After Lin Bin's father had been lost at sea, he became the sole man in the household. When his mother was distressed, he was the only one she could turn to. When his little brother and sister had a fight, or were unruly, it was Lin Bin who dealt with it, arbitrating a way through problems for them.

One day I went for a visit. As soon as I arrived before the window, I saw the family, the four of them, sitting in the parlour in a serious mood. The atmosphere was rather extraordinary, so I stood there outside.

Lin Bin's little brother and sister were seated next to each other on a long bench in a dark nook of the parlour. Lin Bin and his mother were close by. With her headscarf clutched in a hand, his mother was wiping her own tears, now speaking, now silent. Judging from her voice, you would guess she had been provoked into tears. Lin Bin was listening attentively, with a teacup in his hands, deep in thought.

'A-Hui insists that I didn't bring him sea-lavenders on the fifteenth of May, and he is not paying me. I did bring him seventeen and a half catties. He says there's no record in his account book. He's set on abusing us, mother and children… The rice shop people came today and asked for money.'

'He dare not,' Lin Bin's tranquil tone was most like that of his lost father: his small physique, the way he held the teacup, all of these resembled his father. I really couldn't believe it was Lin Bin. 'Who else was in A-Hui's shop that day?' he asked.

'I didn't see anyone. I was reasoning with him all that time, begging him for sympathy.'

'No one outside the shop either?'

Lin Bin's mother contemplated and raised her head, saying: 'Yes! A-Mei saw it, the A-Mei living behind Tianhou Temple. She saw me carrying that bag of sea-lavenders into the shop.'

'Mum, don't cry. Let's go and ask Aunt A-Mei to testify for us.'

At the threshold, Lin Bin turned his head to console his brother and sister. 'Don't be afraid. Mum and I will get the money back. You wait here. Don't go anywhere else. A-Fu, wash the rice. A-Mei, light a fire. Don't be afraid. No one can take advantage of us.'

That calm, reliable Lin Bin, compared with the Lin Bin at school, was almost a completely different person. I couldn't understand; nor could others possibly believe it.

* * *

When we had stabilised the chimneystack with three wooden boards, Wang-Xi, like a sentinel discovering the whereabouts of the enemy, said in a fluster: 'Brother-in-

Law is coming. What should we do?'

We saw Brother-in-Law carrying yellow clay on a shoulder pole and, with tiny steps, trudging painstakingly towards us from the little path. The pole was bent into a bow shape by the heavy clay. The bottoms of the wicker scoops were trailing along the ground, stirring up dust along the way. It appeared that Brother-in-Law would soon be completely overwhelmed by it all.

Outdoing all of us, Ye Ying-San leapt down from the roof of the kiln and dashed over. With a single movement, he took over the shoulder pole and, saying nothing, carried it back, treading bold steps.

'All seven of you are here! And you've erected the chimney?' His head wet with sweat, Brother-in-Law walked behind Ye Ying-San. Seeing us, he was as happy as could be. 'Fantastic! For the opening ceremony today, I've cooked a pot of peanuts, just to celebrate.'

We all grew quite eager. Chun-Hua, Xiang-Zhen, and Touch-Me-Not went to fetch the pot of peanuts. 'Peanuts boiled in salted water—still hot! It's so thoughtful of Mr Tao. Thank you, Sir.'

It was near nightfall, and we were hungry; without minding our manners, we each grabbed a handful of peanuts and cupped them in our hands. Meanwhile, the setting sun, of a reddish-orange colour, cast a slanting light into the workshop; the ray at the door happened to fall upon the entrance to the newly finished kiln. We peeled our peanuts, making crackling noises, as though the kiln had already been lit and were glowing red, with the burning firewood in the kiln-hole also making crackling sounds.

'These tools for pottery making—you've all handled them in the Arts and Crafts class. Would you like me to introduce them again?' Brother-in-Law asked.

'Please teach us while doing it. That would make it easier for us to remember.' Lin Bin went on to ask: 'How long does it take to master pottery making?'

Brother-in-Law stood still in front of the display shelves. I saw the air-dried crude pottery wares that filled the shelves: a gourd-like decanter, a teapot, a tall-stemmed bowl, a fish-shaped letter rack, and a deformed clock. A fretted pen pot, through which shone finely broken rings of light, attracted me most; heaven knew how much hard work Brother-in-Law had put into the pen pot, carving and sculpting it with his tool, stroke after stroke, before the clay went dry. 'To be creative in our daily lives,' Brother-in-Law said, 'we have to spend all our lives learning. Ceramic art is also a matter of live and learn; one can never entirely master it.'

Did he mean to startle us? Hearing this, we couldn't decide whether to believe it or not.

'Sir, why are you making it sound so serious? Now we're afraid of learning it,' Chun-Hua said. 'I thought shaping clay, making things we like, was great fun.'

Brother-in-Law chortled. 'Don't be afraid. Pottery is itself a pleasant creative task. You can mould whatever it is that you love best. Please relax. No need to worry.' Then he hailed Ye Ying-San: 'Please, would you carry inside the clay on the shoulder pole? Let's begin the first step of pottery making: clay screening!'

Ye Ying-San glanced at us and, without a word, walked out in big strides.

Before long, he came back, as asked, carrying the clay on the shoulder pole. I sighed with relief.

But Ye Ying-San's facial expression was not quite right. I was sure the others noticed this too. Those peanuts with which we had celebrated the opening ceremony— he hadn't eaten any of them, standing in a corner of the workshop, as if he were an outsider. Following Brother-in-Law's guidance, he dumped the clay beside the mixing basin and returned to his old place.

Brother-in-Law broke up the raw clay with a spade. A-Pan and I were to do the demonstration. Lin Bin scooped the clay with the spade and moved it onto the mesh screen. A-Pan and I lifted up the sieve and shook it forwards and backwards, to the left and to the right. The sifted clay-dust drizzled down, like sheets of silks and satins. On the mesh screen, there remained only grass roots and stones.

'In pottery making, every single step is crucial. Every step influences whether a work will turn out successful or not,' Brother-in-Law said. 'If we don't remove the debris, we'll face many troubles when we proceed to the next step, kneading the clay.'

Chun-Hua, Touch-Me-Not, and Chen Xiang-Zhen rushed to have a try.

Beaming with pleasure, they set about screening the clay, as if they were sifting out a heap of glutinous rice flour to make preparations for rolling tangyuan and pounding niangao.*

Ye Ying-San came to us and said: 'The kiln has been set up, and the clay has been carried inside. Can I leave?'

At this we all froze. Chen Xiang-Zhen put down the mesh screen and said, frowning: 'What are you rushing away for? We've just begun…'

'I was asked to contribute my labour. Haven't I already done my bit?'

'Who says you're here only to do labour? You're here to learn pottery.'

Ye Ying-San stared at Brother-in-Law. A few moments later, Brother-in-Law said: 'If you work hard, perhaps you'll make the most out of it, unless—that is—you're not interested in clay, unless you don't want to mould it into shapes you like.'

'Sir,' said Chen Xiang-Zhen, 'Ye Ying-San's fingers are powerful and very agile. He's very creative. He'll like it.'

I saw Chun-Hua and Lin Bin swinging their bodies, the corners of their mouths twisted; their faces spelt out disagreement. 'Do you know him better than he himself?' Lin Bin whispered.

'Let him decide whether to join or not,' Brother-in-Law said.

'I… don't care!'

With a jerk of his head, Ye Ying-San walked out of the pottery workshop.

---

* Tangyuan is a ball-shaped sweet made of glutinous rice. Niangao is a cake, also made of glutinous rice, traditionally consumed during Lunar New Year.

6

Debris should be removed from the clay

On the evening of the following day, we went together to the pottery workshop again; but Ye Ying-San and Chen Xiang-Zhen were absent. Everyone noticed this, but none mentioned it.

The clay soaked the previous day in water had become a slurry. Brother-in-Law scooped up handful after handful of it and made lumps to dry on a wooden plank. We sat on both sides of the workbench. Brother-in-Law distributed a small lump of clay to each of us, saying: 'You already know how to knead clay. Press it hard!'

Like kneading dough, we turned the clay over and over, rubbing it. Suddenly, Lin Bin and I both cried out—'Ouch!'—as though we had been stung by bees. 'Is there still gravel in the clay?'

'The debris in the clay hasn't been thoroughly removed,'

Brother-in-Law said as he drew near. He pressed the clay and then carefully split it: 'Two methods. First: put this clay aside, let it dry out, and pulverise and sieve it all over again. Second: carry on the task anyway and pick out the debris as you go on,' he said.

Brother-in-Law smiled and stared, allowing us to make our decisions.

'Let it dry out? How long would that be? It would be too much trouble.' I had a feeling that too long a wait would spoil the pleasure.

'We could go and get more clay,' Chun-Hua said.

'Then we would have to wait till tomorrow, at the earliest. What about now? Sitting here and doing nothing?' Lin Bin said: 'I'm for kneading the clay with extra care and picking out the small stones at the same time; they can't be too numerous.'

'I think so too,' A-Pan said.

Being keen, none of us seemed to want to wait any longer, and Brother-in-Law didn't express any more opinion. We thought about it for a while and began to knead the clay again. We were all careful with our hands, moving gently, as if we were washing our woollen clothes or performing some esoteric ritual. Anyone watching us would have tittered!

Screening clay—the only other option—was really not the most interesting task. That drudgery of shaking it from side to side—who would have had enough patience again for that? To be honest, we burned to start kneading and throwing the clay, to give it final shape and glaze it, send it into the kiln, fire it at the highest temperature, finish the work straight away and bring it home. To enact this process bit by bit, we had to hold down our impulsiveness, squeeze out some patience. But patience which was squeezed out by force was not, after all, real patience.

That the clay contained some debris, preventing us kneading it at will, was of course a nuisance too. But I constantly forgot about it. Pricked here, stung there, I was kneading the clay in a rather daredevil manner.

Before long, there were voices drifting in from outside. We looked over our shoulders.

We saw at once Chen Xiang-Zhen by the door dragging someone's hand. 'What are you making a song and dance about? We're already here. Why don't you come in?' she asked.

We didn't need to look to guess who it was. Who else could it be, if not Ye Ying-San? That strong arm—of all the people at our school, he alone had it. And we were right. Ye Ying-San revealed first one shoulder and one leg. Next, there was half of his face inching into the door space. And then, the entire body began to show itself slowly. Hey! A bride seeing her parents-in-law could hardly be more timid, could she? We were dumbfounded. But once his entire body was there, a drastic change came about. He couldn't be more energetic, swinging towards our workbench like an orangutan, in high spirits and striding awkwardly. Fiercely grabbing a lump of clay, he squeezed himself in beside me. Dong! Once sat down, he got to work kneading his clay vigorously.

For a full three minutes, all of us were watching Ye Ying-San doing his one-man show. He kneaded the clay twenty to thirty times over, making the workbench shake as if by an earthquake. And he erupted in anger: 'Am I a foreigner? What are you looking at?' Only then did we come to ourselves.

Having been shocked into consciousness, Lin Bin dashed the clay in his hands onto the workbench. He too set about imitating an orangutan, a frenzied though clearly smaller one. Pointing at Ye Ying-San with a finger, he was just about to speak when Brother-in-Law stood up and said: 'Save your energy for kneading. Don't fight. Being late, Ye Ying-San must have his excuse.'

'I haven't got any excuse. What excuse do I need?'

Without raising his head, Ye Ying-San carried on kneading his clay with furious force. To accompany this, he began whistling, which was horribly out of tune, as if he were the only person in the workshop, and as if the rest of us—standing, sitting, or staring at him with eyes wide open—were nothing but stupid clay figurines.

I thought Ye Ying-San was going too far! Brother-in-Law spoke up for him, but he was ungrateful, ignoring him and showing such disrespect. One would almost say he was embarrassing Brother-in-Law deliberately. Overlooking that shoddy whistling of his, we yet found him shaking his leg so much that the entire bench became wobbly. I waxed angry, jabbing him with my elbow: 'What are you shaking your leg for?'

'I enjoy shaking it. I'm in a good mood.'

'If you want to shake it, go shake it in front of Tianhou Temple. The pottery workshop doesn't need a spirit medium,' Lin Bin said.

'It's none of your business. We're not at your home,' Ye Ying-San raised his eyebrows and uttered these words with his teeth clenched, putting on a thuggish look. 'I love to shake it here. Anything else to say?'

Even if it was none of our business, surely Brother-in-Law could do something to restrain him?

We looked at Brother-in-Law, waiting to hear his comment. But he was unruffled—that graciousness of manner he had to perfection. With a bitter smile, he gently asked: 'Is something making you feel bad? Did you have a fight with a classmate? Were you punished by someone?'

'I'm fine. Never felt better. Who's got a quarrel with me?'

What was good breeding? Was it like Brother-in-Law, who swallowed every offense, showing no temper even when he was pricked by a needle and stabbed by a knife? I fixed my eyes on Brother-in-Law, waiting to see how, having borne the brunt of Ye Ying-San's insolence, he would respond to it.

Nothing. He kept to his gracious manners, as if nothing had ever happened. He kept to shaking his head, with that bitter smile of his, as if he were appreciating the most engaging scene of a theatrical performance. No more than this. I lowered my head, no longer looking at him, no longer wanting to knead my clay.

'Ye Ying-San, what's all this madness about?' Chen Xiang-Zhen exclaimed.

Her voice hit the walls and was absorbed by the finely porous Laogu stones, becoming in the process so soft as to sound a little quaint. Not satisfied, she rose and unleashed her rebuke: 'Don't be such an ungrateful wretch. What's so special about you? What makes you think you can act in this manner?'

This was strange, I thought: why was it that Ye Ying-San dared not answer back when scolded by Chen Xiang-Zhen?

Ye Ying-San set about kneading his clay desperately—once, twice, three times, and then he simply stood up, kneading it so hard that his head was drenched in sweat, kneading it so hard that you would have thought there was a feud between him and that lump of clay, and he wanted to crush it, reduce it to dust.

I looked at Lin Bin, but Lin Bin turned his head to look at Chun-Hua. Nervously, A-Pan and Touch-Me-Not glanced at me sideways and then stared nervously at Ye Ying-San, who was mindlessly wrestling with his lump of clay. We were all a little alarmed. I could feel it.

Suddenly, Ye Ying-San cried out in pain, as though he had been stung by a jellyfish, withdrawing both hands, bending them in front of his chest, and gaping at that lump of clay.

Blood welled up from the centre of his right palm and trickled down along his wrist. Brother-in-Law lunged forward and pressed Ye Ying-San's wrist with a hand, dragging him to the sink. 'Clean it. We must clean it quickly!'

We were frozen to our seats, and for a while were at a loss for what to say, what to do. Lin Bin bent over to examine that lump of clay, picked out a sharp broken stone and handed it to me. The sherd was glinting, like a fragment of glass.

The three girls crowded to me, and having seen it for themselves, they were as nervous as cats on hot bricks. Chun-Hua dragged Touch-Me-Not around in the workshop, yelling: 'Amitabha! The blood was gushing out. Where's the first-aid kit? Is there a first-aid kit?'

Brother-in-Law, who was cleaning the wound for Ye Ying-San at the sink, told them to go and find it in the bathroom cupboard. The two of them dashed away like chickens with their heads cut off.

Unlike them, Chen Xiang-Zhen tossed her head and walked away, castigating Ye Ying-San while she moved: 'It served you right! You called it on yourself. You're reaping the whirlwind. No remedy for you. You may as well let your blood drain away.'

It surprised me that Chen Xiang-Zhen was behaving this way, that she turned her back and walked towards the front entrance. She covered her face with both hands, wobbling along, but suddenly turned round and came back! With Chun-Hua and Touch-Me-Not, who had brought back bandages and ointment, she dashed to the sink, helping to staunch the blood and treat the wound for Ye Ying-San.

Lin Bin, A-Pan, and I sat down quietly, observing the scene from the workbench. I really couldn't understand it. Did Lin Bin grasp it?

The rosy luminance of the setting sun penetrated the door and the windows. Patch after patch of light attached itself to the workbench and to those finely porous Laogu walls. There was already a chill in the evening air, which wove its way in and out of the workshop. At such a time, ours would have been so lovely and so pleasant a task had we been able to focus on kneading and shaping our clay. Who could have predicted that Ye Ying-San would come and act out this farce, a farce no one understood? And Brother-in-Law tolerated him, came to his defence, and appreciated him even, so much so that the atmosphere in the workshop was completely spoiled. I poked my fingers into the clay and pinched off a small chunk, rubbing it. It was lousy, I thought.

Meanwhile, Ye Ying-San, whose wound had already been bandaged, walked back to the workbench. He stretched his legs apart again and flaunted his index and middle fingers, like a sword, at Lin Bin's nose, demanding: 'Speak! Say, who was playing the dirty trick? Who hid the glass fragment in my clay on purpose?' Then he pointed at me: 'Glasses, it wasn't you, was it?' And then he pointed at A-Pan: 'Was it you? You don't have the guts!'

He confronted three people all at once. This abrupt action both terrified and exasperated us. It also frightened Chen Xiang-Zhen out of her wits. 'Ye Ying-San,' she yelled, 'you're very, very boring. You're hopeless. I put my trust in the wrong person. No one will ever talk to you any more. Get lost!' Chen Xiang-Zhen pressed her hands on her own cheeks and slid her palms over them, apparently wanting to conceal the entire face. She got to her feet and ran out of the workshop.

It seemed that Ye Ying-San was reluctant to let the matter rest. He gave us a black look and then strode out like a lion.

I was thinking: how utterly muddle-headed I was to

have seen in this person a somewhat generous heart, a certain degree of loveliness. He was simply making trouble out of nothing. It would be far too polite even to call him a little bully. I had overestimated him.

'The debris in the clay has to be screened out. Otherwise, in the process of shaping clay, it often happens that you prick yourself or hurt other people.' Was this all? Was this all there was to be said? This was the only comment Brother-in-Law made on this farce whose protagonist had been Ye Ying-San. Why was he not angry? Why didn't he reprimand Ye Ying-San? In giving free rein to Ye Ying-San's insolence, was he trying to cling to his own good manners? Or perhaps at bottom he too was utterly muddle-headed, just like me!

I told everyone I was going home.

Having wrapped my clay in a piece of gauze, I put it in the wooden box under the workbench. Chun-Hua and Lin Bin followed me. A-Pan and Touch-Me-Not did the same. They said good-bye to Brother-in-Law in low voices.

And me? Not wanting to say it, disdaining to say it, refusing to say it, I left in silence.

* * *

For the following few days, I wasn't interested in going to the pottery workshop any more, and I had some ready pretexts. When asked, I simply excused myself by saying that I had a stomach ache, that I was required at home, or that I needed to get back early. At school, I shunned Brother-in-Law when spotting him from afar, no longer wishing to give him the slightest attention.

Every evening, Lin Bin went as usual and dropped in on me at night to make his reports. He said at first that three people had been absent: Ye Ying-San, Chen Xiang-Zhen, and me. Later, Chen Xiang-Zhen came back. The pottery lessons had progressed to throwing, but everyone was quiet. Even though Brother-in-Law made his rounds, giving them individual tuition, the workshop was still enveloped in a desolate mood. The atmosphere was bizarrely dull, so much so that the lessons became less and less interesting.

Chun-Hua had asked about my 'illness'. It was as if she were my personal care-assistant, a sort of professional housekeeper, gently enquiring about my family situations. 'Is there something wrong in your father's business in Taipei? Are you food poisoned? Why do you have a stomach ache everyday?' she asked. She was indeed remarkably patient, bringing up loads of questions, to which I invariably gave the answers 'no', 'dunno', and 'thanks'.

This dragged on until the fourth day, when this care-assistant—my goodness!—became a hag. With her countenance spelling out rage, Chun-Hua blocked my exit at the classroom door. In front of Lin Bin, A-Pan, and Touch-Me-Not, she poured out her rebuke: 'Don't pretend any more. I know it. You don't want to go and learn pottery any more, do you? If you don't, you should let Brother-in-Law know. Dodging around like this—it's scandalous. You're not behaving like a Class Leader!'

'True, I don't want to go. So what?' Having borne the

storm of Chun-Hua's harsh rebuke, I found it difficult to find something less glib to say. I stared at Lin Bin, thinking it must have been this big mouth who had told Chun-Hua about it.

'You must give an excuse. Skulking away without a word like that! Have you no manners? And this when Brother-in-Law has been so kind to us.'

'I want to quit too,' Lin Bin said.

Chun-Hua tilted her head and raised an arrow-like finger at him: 'Why do you always follow him? What excuse have you got for quitting?' Her tone resembled that of a mother at the end of her tether.

'I certainly have got one,' Lin Bin patted his own chest and said. 'Partial! Brother-in-Law has favourites. He's useless. Ye Ying-San was as insolent as that. Everyone saw it. But he wouldn't mouth a single word of reproach. So Ye Ying-San could style himself as a crab, could walk sideways and pinch whomever he wanted to pinch. So he could bark like a mad dog in the workshop, bark until he was happy. Am I being unjust? I'm angry. I don't want to go. What's wrong with that?' Every word of Lin Bin's touched my heart. He spoke well.

Having sustained this fusillade of shouts, Chun-Hua was speechless. Touch-Me-Not Wang-Xi stuck to her silence, glancing at us nervously. A-Pan was busy biting his fingernails, chewing them with relish, as if masticating dried shredded squid. I glared at him, and he spoke: 'I don't quite want to go either. There are already calluses on my palms.'

'This is something no one can force upon you. Don't

want to go? Fine. But you have to say it clearly to Brother-in-Law, to his face,' Chun-Hua said.

'Why bother?' A-Pan said: 'You're bolder than we are. You can tell him for us.'

'Be responsible for your own decisions. Bear the consequences yourself.'

'Sure. What of it?' Lin Bin said. 'I can do it right now.'

* * *

We swung nonchalantly across the playing field, along the walls, and past the incinerator, heading towards the small side entrance. No one spoke on our way there. Any word spoken would have been a waste of breath. Besides, angry people should best restrain their words, lest they say something wrong or their anger flare up as they speak. All of a sudden, we saw Sister walking out of the side entrance. Yes, it was our teacher.

Chun-Hua held us back with her arms: 'Wait! Sister is visiting Brother-in-Law. We'd better stay here for a while.'

We all crowded behind the side entrance, poking out our heads to peep. Why was she here too? Walking out of this side entrance didn't necessarily mean visiting Brother-in-Law, did it?

Sister was carrying a small, blue cloth bag. Looking weighty, it was shaped like a big, tall-stemmed teacup, or like a Chiapao melon—those melons that were well in season now. She took a few steps towards the little path leading to the pottery workshop, hugged the blue bag to her bosom, but then turned abruptly, heading back to the side entrance.

Startled, we jumped to hide, but—gosh—where? The five of us crammed ourselves, one head hitting another, into the incinerator. We resembled five huge lumps of waste for recycling. Daring not make any noise, we listened in silence for a while. But we couldn't hear Sister's steps, and not a soul was in sight. So we all clambered out again and hid at the side entrance to observe.

Immediately we saw Sister walking towards the little path again, in the direction of Brother-in-Law's house. She stopped often—taking three steps forward and then retreating two steps, gazing again and again upon the bag she was carrying. What was she thinking about? What on earth was she intending to do?

Chun-Hua tugged at the tail of my shirt, gesturing that I should be the first to emerge. How would I dare? Sister's movements being so bizarre, she must have been deeply troubled, not wanting others to know. In my opinion, we should leave. We shouldn't visit the workshop that day.

Then, quite unexpectedly, Sister turned resolutely back. This time, she really caught us on the wrong foot: she was walking straight back towards the side entrance.

And by the time we had sensed her direction, it was too late to take shelter again in the incinerator.

We were stopped in our tracks by Sister.

At first she was perplexed, but then she smiled. 'Is there something mysterious hidden in the incinerator?' she asked. 'I was hoping to find you and was sorry that I hadn't come earlier, thinking you were already gone. Thank goodness, you're still here.'

'Are you not visiting Brother-in-Law?' Chun-Hua asked, crying out at once: 'Amitabha! No! No! I thought you were here to visit Mr Tao.'

'There's a bag I'd like to give him. Would you deliver it for me, please?' Sister took a deep breath and handed the blue bag to me, saying: 'It's been wrapped up. Don't unwrap it. Tell him it was I who sent this back.'

I held the bag in both hands and could feel there was a porcelain ware inside—a fretted one, to boot. My heart shuddered! Could this be the pen pot on the display shelf, the one with all those tiny panels cut out? Why did Sister have this? Was it possible that Brother-in-Law had given this to her as a gift and that she thought it ugly, valueless, or ill-shapen?

Sister's face betrayed embarrassment, relief, and compunction, all at once.

Before she left, she reminded me again: 'Chen Yi-Xiong, please handle it well. Don't drop it. And please remember to say Thank You to Mr Tao.'

I was right, I thought. It was that pen pot.

'I wonder what the precious gift inside the bag is, which we can't drop,' Lin Bin said, after Sister had walked away from us out of earshot. 'Please can I have a look?'

'There's nothing to look at. It's their secret,' I refused.

'Secret? If it were a secret, why did she entrust it to us?' Lin Bin asked. 'This is already a semi-public matter. Just one look won't do any harm.'

I held fast: 'If you want a look, wait until we're in the workshop.'

Meantime, Chun-Hua asked: 'What on earth is the

gift?' A-Pan and Touch-Me-Not stretched their necks to stare at the blue bag—obviously they too craved to know what was inside.

If it had turned out that the thing inside was indeed the porcelain pen pot, they would all have guessed that Brother-in-Law had moulded and fired the pen pot by himself and had given it to Sister as a gift, only for it to be rejected by her. In that case, Brother-in-Law would have been even sadder, even more embarrassed, wouldn't he? I couldn't let them see it.

Lin Bin leant forward and circled round me, suddenly thrusting his hand out to snatch it from me.

'A-Bin, stop it!'

But Lin Bin was pulling evil faces, tugging at one end of the cloth bag and clinging obstinately to it, throwing himself into a make-or-break tug-of-war with me. 'A-Bin, stop messing about,' I shouted, holding onto the other end of the bag. Then I made a hard pull, upon which Lin Bin let go of the bag and made me stagger five or six steps backward. Lin Bin dashed to support me, but I missed my footing and tumbled, bottom-first, onto the hard ground of yellow soil. The cloth bag flew out of my grasp, landing far away with a crisp 'clunk'!

I saw Lin Bin gaping. A-Pan was biting his fingernails. Touch-Me-Not tilted her head upon her raised shoulder, fearing to move even an inch. The blue bag unfolded itself, revealing the porcelain fragments. It was over. That was it for Lin Bin; that was it for me.

Chun-Hua squatted to gather the fragments scattered on the ground back into the cloth bag and brought it to me with both hands. 'It's broken. What are you going to do?' Chun-Hua asked.

I was too startled even to be angry. How was I supposed to know what to do? 'Ask Lin Bin!' I said.

'Let's get one thing straight. This is a matter both of us should answer for. You can't blame everything on me,' Lin Bin said. 'Own up and report this to Sister. We've broken the thing. A Class Leader should live up to his image. And I myself should demonstrate a willingness to shoulder my own responsibility. Am I right?'

'No. This is a different matter,' I said. 'I know its original shape. We'll try to glue it up first. Or else, we'll make another one in the same shape.'

'How come you know the shape?' Chun-Hua riveted her eyes on me. Her gaze was too penetrating—it seemed she had fathomed something. 'How do you make another one?' she asked.

'Hmm… don't ask. I just know,' I said. Crumbs, I thought, there was no way out of the pottery lessons now; worse still, we had to make a fretted pen pot surreptitiously. The task was perhaps more difficult than mending a broken net.

Matters were becoming knottier and knottier.

With the cloth bag in her hands, Chun-Hua said again: 'I don't think we can bring this to the workshop today. Let's hide it for the moment.'

We dug a hole under the Laogu wind-fence, buried the bag there, and marked the place with two pieces of dried cattle dung, bits which looked as it happened a little like giant pies. Chun-Hua was right. We had to find another time and place for the gluing and re-making. We couldn't lay everything out on the workbench and crowd together to perform the tasks, could we?

Thanks to all this rumpus, it was already quite late when we arrived at the workshop.

At the entrance, we saw Brother-in-Law hunched over the workbench, with his back turned upon us, like a motionless plaster cast. We approached him, but he didn't take notice.

'Mr Tao,' Chun-Hua called out. 'We're all here, Mr Tao.'

Brother-in-Law turned round. 'You're here,' he said with detachment. He was holding a letter in his hand; with a faint smile on his face, he said again: 'One of my teachers back in the university days wrote. He's coming to Penghu this Saturday. The team includes Professor Lin, a geologist, Professor Song, an archaeologist, and some teaching assistants and students. They hope I can keep them company and show them around.'

'They want you to be their tour guide. Is that why you're worried?' Lin Bin asked.

Brother-in-Law laughed heartily: 'They're not ordinary tourists. They're here to carry out archaeological research. I'm very happy to see my former professor and to hear them talk about their work.'

'Archaeological research?' I asked. 'Is there anything about Penghu that might interest archaeologists?'

'Surely there is, isn't there? Penghu especially abounds with aged people,' Lin Bin said, knitting his eyebrows and squeezing his eyes. His face was comically furrowed with wrinkles. Watching him, A-Pan and Touch-Me-Not giggled. But Chun-Hua scolded him: 'A-Bin, please behave yourself. Don't crack such a cruel joke!'

'I'm not sure about the details of their schedule,' Brother-in-Law said. 'But if you're interested, do come along and ask them in person. Perhaps you know better about certain things than I do. Let Chen Xiang-Zhen and Ye Ying-San know. We'll all go together.'

'Is it possible to do without Ye Ying-San?' Lin Bin asked. 'If it's about carrying things, we can manage pretty well on our own, can we not?'

'He's your schoolmate, and we're all in the same workshop. How can we not invite him?'

'Who's to say he won't do any mischief again!'

'Certainly Ye Ying-San has got some faults. But please forgive him. Give him a chance to improve,' Brother-in-Law said. 'Who hasn't got any faults at all? Lacking confidence, he's just like us.'

Why such a riposte? Lacking in confidence? Who?

'We're kind enough to him,' Chun-Hua snorted. She was also aware—I knew—that Brother-in-Law was a little indulgent towards Ye Ying-San, and not just a little either. We all wanted to say this, but before our words could reach our lips, we swallowed them, not daring to give them utterance, as though a piece of niangao, of a size neither too big nor too small, were stuck in our throats, jammed, not moving either upwards or down. And it hurt.

7

Can I make another one?

Throwing was far more interesting than kneading clay.

Place the clay on the round disc on a potter's wheel, push the treadle to make the disc go round and round, press your fingers into the clay, and little by little it would spin into some sort of shape.

Throwing, though entertaining, required more advanced skills. The rotation of the wheel had to be adjusted to just the right speed. When pressing the clay, you mustn't exert either too much or too little force; otherwise, the clay would become crooked, thick here, thin there, and collapse into a shapeless lump as the wheel turned.

It was necessary to take turns using the two wheels in the workshop. We all thronged around them, impatient to take our turn and try. Lin Bin jostled A-Pan aside, wanting to take my place. But Chun-Hua forestalled him.

'A-Pan, it's your turn. Never yield to anyone. Go,' Chun-Hua said, giving A- Pan a shove. A-Pan stumbled forward and fell squarely onto what had been my seat.

'Why are you teaching him to fall over himself, when there are better things to learn?' Lin Bin protested, with his defiant mouth askew.

'In a queue, whoever comes next should be respected. Why should people let you go first? Those who disregard the queue and muscle their way in to get what they want should be admonished.' Chun-Hua was always straightforward when expressing herself; now she simply raised her voice, addressing herself to A-Pan, who was sitting at the potter's wheel: 'A-Pan, excessive politeness equals cravenness. Excessive modesty resembles diffidence. When your turn comes, never doubt anything whatsoever.'

'Okay, you're quite fluent when scolding people,' A-Bin said, his voice dull.

Meanwhile, Chen Xiang-Zhen had entered, her footsteps soft and silent, and she stood still beside Chun-Hua, with her hands locked in front of her, behaving like a lady, a thoroughly demure one. It looked as if she had turned into a different person than she usually was. She greeted Brother-in-Law gently, her deportment not unlike that of Touch-Me-Not. With that trademark serene expression on his face, Brother-in-Law said lightly: 'Here you are.' Showing no surprise, uttering no reproach, he contemplated and asked: 'Is Ye Ying-San still not coming?'

'He'll come tomorrow.'

Ye Ying-San was really making a bid for the limelight. His arrival was always accompanied by some gimmick. Now, with an eye on the next day, he had sent Chen Xiang-Zhen here to make an announcement ahead of his advent. Wasn't this manoeuvring too much of an artifice?

Hearing this, Lin Bin flew into a rage. He said to Chun-Hua: 'If I should be late tomorrow, please forewarn everyone of this event—when I enter the workshop, everyone must clap. Don't forget it, any of you. Watch closely how I will wrestle with him for the potters' wheels.'

'As a matter of fact, it's useless even if you've monopolised the wheels. See, you've been throwing for several days, but not a shape has come out,' Brother-in-Law said, smiling. 'Before throwing, make sure you have a clear idea of the shape you intend. Draw a sketch in your mind of the form into which you want to mould your clay. Otherwise, when operating the rotating wheel with your foot, you will be nervous and nothing good will come out of your labour.'

'Can we not evolve the shape while throwing?' Lin Bin asked.

'It's not that we can't. But for beginners, the chance of failure is higher, which means more time is required. We've got only two wheels. It wouldn't be fair for anyone to monopolise either of them for a long time.' Brother-in-Law asked A-Pan, who was daydreaming at the wheel: 'Do you know the shape of the ware you would like to make?'

'I can't settle upon any. No idea which is better,' A-Pan said.

Brother-in-Law tilted his heels, pressing A-Pan's shoulder with a hand. 'Take stock of your ability, think about how much store you set by pragmatics and aesthetics, seek inspiration in other people's works, and exercise your own creativity—it's mostly about this.'

'It's beyond me. I'm like a duck listening to thunder, confused.' Lin Bin frowned and shrugged, turning his head to ask me: 'Glasses, can you think of any shape?'

I could grasp bits and pieces of what Brother-in-Law meant. Before throwing at the potter's wheel, we should have had a tentative plan or a rough sketch. We couldn't depend on luck alone—on 'crossing the bridge when coming to it' or 'playing it by ear'—which might prove to be a waste of time. There was some truth in what he said. It was only that this tentative idea—this creative sketch— was so hard to achieve.

I made my way to the workbench and sat down on the long seat.

With their clay cupped in both hands, Lin Bin and Chun-Hua joined me and sat down. Meanwhile, Chen Xiang-Zhen—she who had transformed herself into a lady—perched herself nearby, absent-mindedly jabbing her clay with a finger and then withdrawing it. Apparently she wanted to say something, but seeing no opportunity, she only opened her mouth and then closed it again.

So I asked: 'Is he coming tomorrow?'

Chen Xiang-Zhen nodded.

'This little bully is really putting on airs. The captain of an ironclad ship wouldn't be as cocky as he is,' Lin Bin said, forcing air through his nostrils.

'Mr Lin, please don't speak of him like that. He's not as bad as everyone imagines,' Chen Xiang-Zhen began to speak. 'He's sometimes very kind. He's sometimes very caring. He…'

'He, he, who's he?' Lin Bin asked. 'Is it not enough that Brother-in-Law is indulgent towards him? Do you need to join the ranks of patronage too? Very well. Let's all pamper him, make a fuss, lionise him, deify him, send Big Brother Ye Ying-San into heaven. Come on!'

'Why are you using such reckless language? Send him into heaven?' Chun-Hua stopped him. 'Brother-in-Law must have his reasons. Don't embarrass him by such words. Please speak less loudly.'

'Ye Ying-San is really not that bad. He's not like that at home. Really.'

'I'm sure he's not, because someone would punish him at home,' Lin Bin said.

'It happens to be the opposite.' Chen Xiang-Zhen lowered her head, moistened her lips with her tongue, swallowed hard, and said: 'I shouldn't be talking about Ye Ying-San's family, but I don't want you to be wrong about him. We're neighbours—his house is right behind where I live. At home, he has to do plenty of chores—cooking, laundry, taking care of his younger siblings, and looking after their pigs. Ye Ying-San is a dutiful brother.'

'And his parents?' I asked. 'Can he handle so many things alone?'

'His father is a fisherman, seldom at home. Mrs Ye passed away when he was very little,' Chen Xiang-Zhen said. 'He doesn't want his friends to visit his house and see him so frantically busy. He's very meek at home. I don't know why he acts like this when he's out. Really.'

Chun-Hua moved close to her and asked gently: 'Is it really so?'

'Please don't think he's rude and cut him off.' It seemed that Chen Xiang-Zhen would start crying. 'Please forgive him. Please.'

I was sure that Chen Xiang-Zhen was not fabricating the story. But it was also true that Ye Ying-San's insolence and insouciance, his rudeness and recklessness, were a far cry from what she was describing. I had imagined he had had an excessively indulgent and pampering family. Who would have guessed the truth was quite the opposite?

'Why are you so kind to Ye Ying-San? Speak!' Lin Bin asked. 'What right has he got to treat us like this?'

Lin Bin was right. Even if Ye Ying-San was from a broken family, did that mean he had a right to do mischief with impunity? We were all happy to support him, but he was not entitled to special tolerance. While he was perpetrating misdeeds, surely we shouldn't exercise extra forbearance, let alone find excuses and claim privileges for him, as if everyone were responsible for the misfortunes his family had undergone.

'We're classmates, and we grew up together,' Chen Xiang-Zhen said. 'The day Ye Ying-San's mother passed away, my mother and I rushed there and saw her take her last breath. She asked us to look after him whenever possible. Mother agreed. So did I. That year, Ye Ying-San and I were both eight years old. Thank you.'

All this time, Brother-in-Law had been at the sink in a corner of the workshop, busying himself with washing and rubbing. Did those few tools take so much time to wash?

I wondered whether he had overheard our conversation.

And what exactly was Chen Xiang-Zhen thanking us for?

Chun-Hua and Touch-Me-Not held their peace. Lin Bin was cracking his knuckles. Everyone stared at me, apparently wanting me to speak.

'It's quite late. Let's go home to think about the shapes of our pottery wares,' I said. 'To be fair, not every one of us has a happy family life. Am I right? But if he wants to be tolerated, he should change himself for the better. I don't think Ye Ying-San has any right to do mischief. That's the point.'

Having said this, however, I no longer held a grudge against Brother-in-Law and Chen Xiang-Zhen for being partial. Though I still thought Ye Ying-San was going too far, I didn't loathe him any longer. The only thing that still puzzled me was why he needed to put on such a brash front in public.

We sank into silence. I couldn't tell what was on their minds.

* * *

Throughout the day, we dared not talk with Sister. We avoided her, afraid that she might ask us about the fretted pen pot. I kept the mood as light as I could, feigning ignorance. A-Pan adhered to his usual smiling, polite demeanour. Touch-Me-Not always being nervous, no one could detect any difference now anyway.

Lin Bin and Wu Chun-Hua were different, however.

Their faces went all to pieces when they spotted Sister—especially Lin Bin, who dared not look straight at Sister, dodging here and there instead. You knew immediately there was something wrong! Sister asked him several times: 'Did you forget to bring your textbooks again?' 'Did you break the windows again?' We felt nervous for him.

This day, Lin Bin brought his super glue to school. During the lunch break, we returned to the Laogu wind-fence outside the small side entrance and dug out the cloth-wrapped broken pen pot. Oh crumbs! Where would we begin to glue it back together? We couldn't even tell which was the base and which was the middle. We sat on the dried cow pats, trying to patch together the fragments: piece after piece, we picked them up, applied the glue and blew it dry painstakingly; after no end of trying this and trying that, we had managed only to glue up the oval neck of the pen pot. But how could we glue the entire work together? The more I thought about it, the more I marvelled at my own stupidity.

'Glasses, are you sure you can glue it together?' Lin Bin asked.

'You?'

'Me? I'm asking you.'

All of a sudden, I heard footsteps approaching from the little path behind us. I pulled back my feet quickly and turned my head to look through an aperture between the stones. It was Brother-in-Law! Apparently he had sensed that someone was behind the wind-fence. While walking, he bent his back and looked in our direction.

I hastened to wrap up the fragments of the pen pot,

thrusting Lin Bin away, and attempting to bury the cloth bag back into the hole. But Lin Bin shouted: 'What now? Bitten by a big ant?'

It was too late. Brother-in-Law had already arrived at our side. I rose swiftly.

Lin Bin too was so shocked that he bounced to his feet.

'It's you two? Why are you out here? I thought you'd be taking a nap?' He asked, fixing his eyes firmly on mine.

'Eh… Yes, we're out here to muse on the shapes.' I stretched one leg slowly out, pushing the cloth bag behind my heels to hide it from view. But the cursed fragments made a snapping sound, which frightened Lin Bin into opening his mouth. I hurried to ask him: 'What are you here for?'

'Me? The same as you.' He moved closer, putting the super glue in his hand back into his pocket, trembling all over. 'It's so mind-tasking, not easy at all to think of a shape,' he added.

Once again, Brother-in-Law looked us all over, his eyes dwelling on my heels, for a moment or two, and then on Lin Bin's pocket, for two more seconds. He tilted his heels and said: 'Good. If you can think of a shape, it will be easier for the work in the evening.' He took a few steps and stopped: 'Just to let you know some good news first—my professor's archaeology team has arrived in Penghu. They will begin work on the Isle of Jibei this Saturday. We can camp there during the visit.'

'Fantastic!' Lin Bin's excitement seemed over the top. Brother-in-Law was strange too. We had already known this matter. Why did he announce it as 'good news' in so serious a manner? He took two steps, slowed down, and then made his way towards the small side entrance.

I heaved a sigh of relief and said: 'Too dangerous. He almost found it out.'

Lin Bin's face had relaxed and was completely normal again. Now, with contempt, he uttered these words: 'Dangerous? What? We might as well have handed over the fragments with the bag and told him the truth; that is, we had broken Sister's gift for him. He probably would have kept them as a memorial, as a treasure. Why did you have to be so nervous? It was contagious.'

'No way. Brother-in-Law would have been sad and angry.'

'What makes you think like that?' Lin Bin asked. 'You clearly don't know him very well. Brother-in-Law is never angry.'

* * *

In the evening, Ye Ying-San turned up, just as predicted. Moreover, he had got there earlier than the rest of us, sitting opposite Chen Xiang-Zhen and toiling away at the workbench.

With smiling eyes, Chen Xiang-Zhen greeted us. That warm-heartedness was a radical departure from her habitual image. Ye Ying-San was even quainter, sticking out a hand and saying 'Hi' to us. He demonstrated not so much a jolly mood as a touch of madness. Surely you wouldn't behave like this even when meeting a friend after a long absence? Alarmed by the atmosphere, Touch-Me-

Not hid behind Chun-Hua, and A-Pan behind my back. We halted at the entrance to the workshop and stood there for a while. Then, Lin Bin took a stride sideways, cleared his throat very loudly, and said: 'What are you afraid of? Let's go!'

Casting our eyes around, we made our way to the workbench and returned greetings to Ye Ying-San and Chen Xiang-Zhen. I had imagined that Ye Ying-San, having come back to the workshop, might have shown some signs of repentance or embarrassment at least, quite apart from moderating his cockiness. As it turned out, however, he exuded perfect confidence, like a world-famous football player who, having been ejected because of a flagrant foul, returned to the pitch after a few days, suddenly waxing polite and taking the initiative to wave at the spectators: you couldn't decide whether to be angry or to applaud. Consumed with bashfulness, we were no match for him.

'All of us are here again? Jolly good,' Brother-in-Law said. 'This evening, we are to exercise our creativity. Each of us should mould our clay into the shape we fancy. Please begin.' Brother-in-Law's jovial mood breathed into the workshop an unwonted air of harmony and happiness.

I had already thought of a plan: a teapot and six small teacups made of our hometown's clay, for my father to use in Taipei—perhaps he would like them. I wanted to mould the teapot into an octagonal shape, which would be reminiscent of Penghu's Guanyin Pavilion. Would I succeed? I wondered.

Chun-Hua wanted to make a pair of porcelain pillows

for her parents.

'Do you want them to have stiff necks everyday?' Lin Bin asked.

'I'll measure the proportions properly. No worries. My grandmother has a porcelain pillow, which is ice-cold and very comfortable to rest your head on.' Chun-Hua burst into giggles and tossed the question back to Lin Bin: 'What magnificent work are you going to make?'

Lin Bin turned a deaf ear, asking Brother-in-Law instead whether there was any limitation on the sizes of the wares. Brother-in-Law replied that as long as his work was not too heavy to carry, and as long as the kiln could accommodate it, he could make whatever he wanted. Hearing this, Lin Bin declared: 'I'm going to make a rice vat! What do you think?'

A gale of laughter swept across the workshop, blowing us off our balance.

Discombobulated were we! 'Do rice vats need to be designed too?'

'Don't laugh. This is not an ordinary rice vat.' Lin Bin was so flustered that every bit of his face was red. 'There's going to be an outlet at the bottom of the vat. You won't need a scoop for the rice. There's also a copyright component for keeping away cockroaches and rats. Copyright, mind you!'

Lin Bin's rice vat was not special enough to take the biscuit. We would never have guessed that what the timid Touch-Me-Not Lin Wang-Xi wanted to make was a toilet for his little brother. Toilet? Hearing this, we all burst into a riot of laughter again.

Chun-Hua tapped on the workbench and asked: 'What's

so funny about that? Have you, like Wang-Xi, thought of making something for your little brothers or sisters?'

We all shut up, not daring to laugh any longer. In a calm, serene tone of voice, Chen Xiang-Zhen said: 'I want to make a pair of piggy banks. Big ones.'

'What for?' Lin Bin asked.

'For saving money, to buy a ship in the future.'

'You'll be saving until when? Twenty piggy banks wouldn't be enough for that.'

A-Pan was scratching his head and pressing his ear, looking rather troubled. 'Sir, I can't make up my mind which shape is better. Can you all think of one for me, please?'

Who knew what he would like? How were we supposed to think of a shape for him? Brother-in-Law said: 'No. Put more thought into it. You'll have to make your own choice. Don't expect others to come up with an idea for you. Try. Try harder.'

'And I want to make a clay figurine, the like of which has never been seen before. This evening, you're all very, very privileged,' Ye Ying-San said, shaking one leg and swinging his body. His body language suggested a mood of relaxation that bordered on nonchalance. 'Listen. This clay man will be myself.' As he said this, he set about laughing, in spite of all of us.

'That's also fine. Give free rein to your creativity. As long as you are faithful to your heart in turning the clay into the shape you fancy, it will be a good work.' Brother-in-Law clapped. 'Alright. Shall we begin?'

'I'll put my rice vat aside for the time being. I also

want to make a clay figurine, and that figurine will also be myself. It will bring good luck to anyone who sees it.' Lin Bin had already taken over one of the potters' wheels, but having heard Ye Ying-San's plan, he returned to the workbench.

What was Lin Bin up to? He seemed intent upon competing with Ye Ying-San, even upon becoming his nemesis. He passed the other seats, sat down deliberately opposite to Ye Ying-San, and started to mimic that out-of-tune whistling of his.

We were happy, busy, one and all. Chun-Hua and I went up to the potters' wheels first; the others sat around the workbench. Brother-in-Law made his rounds, priming the tools and offering guidance here and there. He stopped at my side, bent his back, and said: 'Push the treadle steadily. Do it step by step. The pressure you put on the treadle should be even. This is one of the basics. It calls for some application.'

I was clutching and pressing the clay on the rotating disc. I found it hard to keep the rotational speed even while the pressure exercised by my hands was forever varying. It was difficult enough to achieve hand-and-foot coordination, but on top of this, you also had to pay attention to the moistness and the evolving shape of the clay.

Chun-Hua, who was moulding her clay into a cylindrical shape, asked: 'Does the rotational speed have to be even?'

'Throwing at an uneven speed can create a certain effect,' Brother-in-Law explained, 'but for beginners, I would suggest making it even. This is basic training.'

'I'd like to make it rotate faster. May I?' I asked.

'Yes, give it a go.'

'I'd like to move it more slowly, lest my work should fall in on itself,' Chun-Hua said.

'Yes, give it a go.'

Being so encouraging, and granting us complete freedom to put our ideas into practice, Brother-in-Law was nevertheless making us a little nervous. It was as though we had sailed out, all alone, on a sampan—unrestrained by anyone, we yet had to take full responsibility for our actions. Inevitably, I was at once excited and flustered, so flustered that my hands and feet were running away from me.

At the workbench, nevertheless, there was unbroken singing, accompanied by Lin Bin's and Ye Ying-San's shoddy whistling. It was such a cheerful scene! Chen Xiang-Zhen was forever prompting A-Pan: 'More loudly please. You're the best singer. Don't be shy.'

Ye Ying-San whistled and laughed alternately. I wondered why he was so happy. This person was indeed strange—he could alter his demeanour at the drop of a hat. And when this happened, the difference was colossal, taking him beyond recognition.

Shaking his body, he held up the clay figurine he had made, swung over in front of me, and asked: 'Glasses, look closely. Does this look like me?'

It was a big monster that resembled both an orangutan and a bear—pursed mouth, thick lips, tiny ears, and hanging arms—as if it were bellowing and dashing forward. Ye Ying-San certainly knew what he was doing. While we, extremely busy, were not even halfway through our work, he had already finished his clay figurine with great facility. Above all, the monster's forehead wrinkles and dishevelled hair were all really finely delineated. It was surprising that such strong arms as Ye Ying-San had could actually govern such exceptionally nimble and refined fingers.

He then showed Chun-Hua the clay figurine, asking: 'Look closely. Does this look like me?' Ye Ying-San made an elegant move: resting one hand on his waist, with the figurine in the palm of the other hand, mincing around, drawing a few circles in the air with his protruding arm, and then giving the figurine pride of place at the centre of the workbench. Laughing, he made this introduction: 'This is the little bully Ye Ying-San. If you've never dared to look him in the eye, now's your chance. He looks nice, doesn't he?'

Ye Ying-San's series of actions left me a little ill at ease. We all stared at him in embarrassment. It felt as if the workshop were suffused with choking smoke. The original jovial mood was suddenly all gone.

Lin Bin cleared his throat and said: 'What's so special about your clay figurine? Look at this Monkey King I've made. This is me. What do you think?'

Meanwhile, Brother-in-Law made his way to the workbench slowly. He pointed at Ye Ying-San's monstrous clay figurine and asked: 'Why did you make this thing?'

'Are we not allowed to make whatever we want? This is myself.'

Brother-in-Law's face grew pale, his finger trembling. 'Why is it in such a shape?' he asked again.

'He is me, and I am him' Ye Ying-San replied, smiling.

Chun-Hua and I leapt up from the potters' wheels. It was terrifying to see the pallor of Brother-in-Law's face, which looked like a faded wall newspaper. He clenched his teeth, the muscles on his cheeks now tense, now relaxed. The evening breeze and the glow of the setting sun in the workshop seemed to be clenched between his teeth this way. Everything was still.

Suddenly, he thrust out a hand, sweeping the clay figurine away with so much force that you would have imagined he had come face to face with a fierce wild beast. The figurine turned a few somersaults on the workbench and flew out, crashing headfirst into a corner of the wall. It broke into atoms!

Chun-Hua grasped my elbow. Touch-Me-Not let out a terrified cry. And then the workshop sank back into profound silence. Next, I heard my own breathing, like the tidal noises in the Fenggui Blowholes, deep and yet clear—it felt as if the workshop were also full of those tidal echoes.

Ye Ying-San's smile had vanished. He shot up from the bench, clenching his fists, and trembling too. His mouth was open, but it gave no voice. He stared daggers at Brother-in-Law, and we gazed upon him—standing or sitting, all of us seemed to be frozen. Even time appeared to have stopped.

There was a rumbling noise in my ears. My head seemed to be swelling continuously, but I couldn't remember anything. We had begun so well, hadn't we? Why had it suddenly turned into this? Why was Brother-in-Law so angry? Wasn't he a well-tempered, well-mannered person, after all?

'I can forgive you when you make a mistake, and I can allot you time to put it right,' Brother-in-Law strode in front of Ye Ying-San. I was really worried that Ye Ying-San might lose his mind and take a swipe at Brother-in-Law. 'But you don't do yourself justice,' he continued. 'Do you really want to be like that clay figurine, keeping that savage look frozen in perpetuity? Why do you think of yourself this way?' Brother-in-Law's voice was trembling, his face a ghastly pallor, and the corners of his eyes convulsing. He gasped these words out, as if he had been punched in the chest and had been trying to suppress his pain: 'Is that really how you see yourself? Answer me! And do you think your friends have an obligation to endure your wild temper? Do you? You never notice other people's good will, do you? Once a mistake is committed, you want to go on with it forever and ever? Do you? Answer me.'

Ye Ying-San was like a mackerel out of water, opening his mouth to gasp, but incapable of breathing out a single word.

'Whose is this obligation always to indulge you? You're disgracing yourself to such an extent that you're hell bent on hurting others, harming yourself. Am I right about you? Answer me.'

Ye Ying-San's fists were still tightly clenched. I couldn't tell whether it was because he was so enraged that he was trembling, or was it only with so much force that he could gain control over his trembling? He turned his head towards that heap of smashed clay in the corner, his eyes riveted upon it, motionless. Meanwhile, Chen Xiang-Zhen pushed her hands against the workbench and stood up. But she lowered her head and hunched her shoulders, making her way towards the corner, her pace ever so slow. I wondered why. None of us knew why. She pressed her hand to her mouth, but sobbing sounds escaped from her nostrils. Her hair flopped down over her eyes. I couldn't make out whether she was shedding tears or whether her eyes were closed.

Having reached the corner, Chen Xiang-Zhen squatted and, contrary to everything we had expected, began to pick up the clay fragments, one by one, lodging them carefully in her palm. She was so gentle, seeming to fear that just a bit of force might break them once again.

I stared, stared mesmerised. All the while, she was working silently and attentively, like a woman picking crowned turban shells when the tide was low in Penghu Bay.

Chun-Hua raised her head, took a deep breath, and made her way to the corner too. She joined Chen Xiang-Zhen, picking up the fragments scattered over the floor and placing them in the palm of her hand. The setting sun outside the window blazed upon their backs, the light so dazzling that nothing could be made out for certain. I blinked again and again, only to find my sight all the more blurred.

They brought the fragments, which were cupped in their hands, and laid them on the workbench. Then they slipped back into the corner.

Quite out of the blue, Brother-in-Law stuck out a hand

and swept those fragments onto the floor again. There was a tightening sensation in my heart. I couldn't help trembling. What happened to Brother-in-Law? Being so cruel, was he not afraid that he might destroy not just Ye Ying-San's figurine, but also the very person who had made it? He would, he would, he would destroy Ye Ying-San. How could he do that? How could he sweep away those fragments a second time?

Startled, Chen Xiang-Zhen and Chun-Hua almost leapt aside, once again squatting on the floor to pick up the fragments, now scattered all over the place. They laid them, one after another, in their palms. A-Pan and Touch-Me-Not followed suite and left their seats, moving to the heap of clay that had been broken into smithereens. Over and over again, they scraped the floor with their hands and brought the pulverised clay back to the workbench. My entrails seemed to be rubbing violently against each other, as though they were stirred together. It was so painful that I wanted to contract my body, wanted to sit down, so painful that I was dizzy, covered in a cold sweat, feeling nauseous.

Then, to our consternation, with a single strike, Lin Bin crushed the Monkey King he had made on the workbench, rubbing the fragments against each other again and again. Gosh! Everyone was going crazy. We were like strangers, strange, deranged people. Gripping my stomach, I sat down beside the potters' wheels, eyeing Ye Ying-San walk and stop, and walk and stop again, but still making his way, half walking and half running, towards Chen Xiang-Zhen.

Ye Ying-San picked up the fragments of his figurine and cupped them in his hands too.

He brought them back, heaped them on the workbench, and walked towards Brother-in-Law. I saw him open his mouth. 'Sir, can I make a new one, please? May I?' he asked.

Then it was my turn to gasp. I gulped, and held my breath, incapable of making any sound. Gazing upon the scene in the workshop, I tried hard to keep my eyes wide open but still couldn't get a clear view. Everything before my eyes resembled the landscape one would see through a window lashed by rain, a landscape drenched and dripping, trance-like and blurred.

Only the persistent patter of the rain penetrated the workshop through the skylight in the roof, seeped in through the finely porous Laogu walls, and rose from the floor bespattered with clay dust. With the drizzling rain, the sound pervaded the air and the earth, suffused the earth and the air, bent only upon burying us.

'May I?'

Why didn't Brother-in-Law answer him?

8

Sherds on Jibei Beach

On Saturday, the Ye family's boat was waiting for us at Magong Port.

Ye Ying-San and his father stood by the boat, helping us aboard one by one.

Chen Xiang-Zhen—as if a member of the Ye family—arrived fairly early too and was busy greeting us, showing us the way, and settling everything.

'No need to sit down, really. Boys and girls, come learn fishing. Youngsters in Penghu should know how to fish. Who doesn't? Come. I'll teach you,' a fisherman whom we called Uncle Shun-Li said, with a smile on his face, his arms akimbo. 'Especially Ying-San, because you are about five feet and a half tall and weigh more than nine stone. Such a build—it'll be a real pity if you don't come on board and do some fishing.'

'They're all swots. Who would go for fishing?' Ye Ying-San's father said. 'Call it a success if they get away without the fish catching them!'

'What's wrong with being swots? They're intelligent, so they'll catch more fish. Good at maths, they won't make counting errors. Such talents are most welcome on board.'

'Ying-San, what's your plan? Do you want to share it with us?' Uncle Shun-Li asked. Ye Ying-San stood beside the helm in the wheelhouse; he could manage nothing but an embarrassed smile.

Brother-in-Law spoke: 'Mr Ye, thank you so much for agreeing to make a detour and for giving us a lift to Jibei. I would like to say Thank You on behalf of my students.'

'You mustn't stand on ceremony. To be honest, even though I've always been happy to be at your service, there's hardly ever been a chance to do that.' Ye Ying-San's father was controlling the helm. The fishing boat chugged out of the port towards the open sea, and the sounds of the wind and the waves grew louder. Raising his voice, he pronounced: 'Ying-San is a good boy at home. I don't know what he's like at school. If he misbehaves, Sir, don't be polite to him. Punish him as you see fit. Overindulgence would do him no good.'

Once we had left the harbour behind us, three dolphins approached. They were diving, porpoising, rolling, and making sounds—sounds akin to the cute gurgling of infants—beside the boat. They also brought to mind water ballet performers, crisscrossing each other above the water ahead of the boat, making every effort to earn some warm applause from us. They made us laugh so hard.

'Blimey! You haven't even seen dolphins before? You fake Penghu people.' Looking at us, Uncle Shun-Li appeared disgruntled. With a bitter smile, he shook his head. Brother-in-Law and Ye Ying-San's father were talking in the wheelhouse about our school; together with Ye Ying-San, we migrated to the stern to gain a better view without being laughed at.

Two hours later, the boat reached Jibei Port. 'The Yongmanzai* will be casting nets near Jibei. This time tomorrow, we'll come and fetch you,' Ye Ying-San's father said. Then, turning towards the stern, he shouted: 'Ying-San, be more lively when you're outdoors. Don't act as if you were still at home—so bashful, so timorous, not daring to say Hello to people. Be more cheerful!'

Who on earth was he referring to? Was Ye Ying-San ever not lively, not cheerful enough? Was he ever bashful and timorous?

Hearing this, we really couldn't help bursting into another bout of laughter.

* * *

We were on dry land once more, but the archaeology team were nowhere to be seen.

We made our way to the square before Sietian Temple, which was right in front of the port. Three lanes were seen

---

* The name of the boat literally means 'always full of catch'.

on the left, another three on the right, and the houses built of Laogu stones were all of the same structure. It was as though we were standing at the starting point of a labyrinth, and we didn't have a clue which of the lanes we should take.

On the map, Jibei seemed a small enough isle. But not until we had set foot on the isle did we realise how uneven and convoluted its topography was and how complicated the configuration of its houses and lanes seemed. If you didn't keep your wits about you, you would perhaps lose your way. We kept our backs straight, craned our necks, and looked here and there. Lin Bin stood at the top of the stone steps, taking in a panorama of what lay around him. 'Quite a few houses, but not many people are in sight,' he reported. 'Let's do it this way. We'll play rock-paper-scissors. The winner chooses a road. It's very fair, isn't it?'

Lin Bin was too ridiculous. This literally meant making a wild guess. And he was prattling on about being fair!

With her head tilted and one shoulder raised, the bashful Wang-Xi breathed out these words gently: 'May I? May I ask at the village store there, please?'

Touch-Me-Not taking the initiative to ask something? Her courage amazed everyone. She shuffled away. Gazing upon her back, Lin Bin spoke again: 'Touch-Me-Not is not to be trifled with. Ye Ying-San's father said: "Be more lively when you're outdoors," and she picked it up at once.'

What came next was even more amazing.

Before long, we spotted Touch-Me-Not on her way back from the village store, and there was a little boy at her side, who was calling her in a sweet voice: 'Sis Wang-Xi, Sis

Wang-Xi!' The boy was running around her, apparently reluctant to go away, in response to which Touch-Me-Not took his hand and caressed his head—you couldn't have shown more affection.

This came as another shock, knocking us nearly for six. Who of us was so capable as to adopt a little brother after just a few seconds in a village store? Even Lin Bin and Chun-Hua—reputedly the most outgoing amongst us—could probably not boast of such an achievement, not to mention the rest of us.

'Sis Wang-Xi, Mum wants to make red tortoise cakes for all of you. Those that were made on Mazu's birthday* have all been eaten up. My belly was this big,' the boy said loudly. Having seen us, he asked: 'Are these your teacher and classmates? When I grow up, I want to have many teachers and classmates too, this many, this old, this big.'

Wang-Xi was indeed not to be trifled with. Once round the village store, and she had already found a new brother and—what was more—had herself been adopted by a mother! And thanks to her, we were going to have red tortoise cakes! Surely we had underestimated her.

Wang-Xi said: 'The archaeology team has been here for many days—they're near the big Wooden Fish on the eastern coast. I know that place. My little brother is coming with us too.' That boy added: 'They're all carrying sacks, picking at broken bowls and jars everyday. Dad says they're an idle bunch, they're all from Taipei.'

---

* Mazu is a patron goddess worshipped in some coastal regions in East Asia and Southeast Asia.

'Wang-Xi, how come you're so capable?' Lin Bin asked.

Wang-Xi was still wearing that diffident look: 'Oh, but I'm not!'

'Sis Wang-Xi has always been very capable. She can mend broken nets too,' the boy thrust his chest out and said. 'I'll fight a duel with whoever bullies her!' And with these words, he began to brandish his little fists, performing a Chinese boxing movement whose name eluded us—it seemed very powerful indeed.

Brother-in-Law said nothing, smiling there like an outsider. As though we were swept by the force of the boy's fists, we scattered ourselves, backing up to the top of the stone steps. 'Wang-Xi, this little prince—your adopted brother—can play a role in a wuxia* film, the male lead,' I said.

'He's my cousin, my uncle's son. He started to learn Shaolin Boxing as soon as he could walk.'

'Why didn't you tell us earlier? How many times have you been to Jibei?'

'It's impossible to tell. I lived here when I was little,' Wang-Xi said timidly. 'I was here too last week, on Mazu's birthday.'

Feeling as if we had been tricked, we exclaimed in unison: 'Why didn't you say that? Why didn't you tell us earlier?' So the lady running the village store was actually her aunt, wasn't she? From the moment we were told about this trip to Jibei, to boarding the boat and coming

---

* Wuxia is a genre that features adventures of Chinese martial artists.

ashore, and then to our finding ourselves at a loss, she had remained silent, trailing at the tail of the group. She had appeared to be someone from far away, even more so than a common tourist. 'You're so good at pretending,' I said.

'I'm not pretending. No one asked.'

'And we were all at sixes and sevens! You should have told us much earlier that this is your hometown!'

'Jibei is very small. We won't get lost.'

The boy let out a cry, acted out a kung-fu move, and let fly a few punches against the sky, at which we all shut up and covered our mouths. He put on a leonine expression, pressed against me and said: 'How dare you bully Sis Wang-Xi! Take my punch!'

Wang-Xi dashed and grabbed his shoulder, admonishing him: 'He's our Class Leader. You can't do that.'

The boy appeared to be stunned by the title 'Class Leader'. But although his swelling aggressiveness relented a little, he went on to reassure Wang-Xi: 'Sis, don't be afraid. I'm right here. Is a class leader greater than a prince?'

Meanwhile, Brother-in-Law yawned and stretched his arms and legs, as if he had just finished watching a little bit of theatre. He clapped three times and said: 'Have you had enough fun? Let's follow Wang-Xi and this kung-fu boy and meet up with the archaeology team.'

* * *

On the shining white beach was a vast wooden fish. In contrast to the seawater, which was emerald green, the brilliantly red wooden fish stood out prominently, looking like a fortress but painted in the wrong colour.

A wooden fish was used during the recitation of Buddhist scriptures. Why was this one so big? And why was it placed by the sea—rather than in the Guanyin* temple—and thus exposed to the elements? Wang-Xi said: 'This is a treasure that can appease the wind and ward off evil spirits. On the opposite coast of Jibei, there's another one, a Bronze Bell, which is as big as the Wooden Fish.'

A Wooden Fish and a Bronze Bell—wouldn't the tapping of the one and the chiming of the other be heard throughout all of Penghu's isles?

'You can't strike it without permission. Only when there's an important event—and when the Chief of the Village permits—are people allowed to strike it.'

'What incredibly important events?'

'For example, pilgrimage processions in honour of Mazu, village meetings, fires, and...' Wang-Xi faltered. It suddenly dawned upon us—we knew what other thing would make them take the trouble to send somebody to strike the Bell and the Wooden Fish. Such a thing was inauspicious, and we were forbidden, by grownups, from mentioning it unless there was a good reason. But the kung-fu boy bounced forward and said: 'It's when a boat is turned upside down, the fisherman falls into the sea and is about to meet his maker—so everyone in Jibei can come to his rescue. You don't even know this!'

Ah, this boy knew way too much. And he was too

---

* Guanyin is the deity of mercy, worshipped throughout East Asia.

talkative.

Lin Bin pulled out one or two hairs from his head, attempting to tease him.

The boy's eyes flashed exasperation; as soon as he had spotted the hand and found out who the criminal was, he flaunted his little fists and legs and set about beating Lin Bin with all his force. Chased, Lin Bin looked as if he were in flight, circling us round and round. We tuned a blind eye and ignored Lin Bin's cries—let them have fun fighting!

* * *

As expected, we found six or seven people with sacks on their backs close to the big Wooden Fish; bending over, they were searching. Brother-in-Law had already broken into a run, calling out while he was dashing: 'Professor Song, Professor Song…'

Like a herd of goats, we bounced over those ditches in the peanut fields and dashed towards the coast, following Brother-in-Law. Those six or seven people with sacks on their backs rose and rubbed their waists, waving at us with smiling faces. Not unexpectedly, all of them had sherds in their hands. The kung-fu boy said: 'See, I didn't lie. They're picking broken bowls and broken jars to fill their bags. My dad said, they…' Wang-Xi hastened to grab him; Ye Ying-San covered his mouth. The kung-fu boy twisted his body. Unable to release himself from Ye Ying-San's hand, he bit him. It was so painful that Ye Ying-San leapt aside and asked: 'Does Shaolin Boxing teach you this biting movement?'

'Hello and welcome. This little boy was the first Jibei local we met. Outgoing and inquisitive, he could be an outstanding journalist one day. The day we arrived in Jibei, he volunteered to be our guide. We gave him some dried food to eat, but he said no—he wanted red tortoise cakes. But we couldn't supply him with any, could we?' The middle-aged man had grey hair around his temples. He was Brother-in-Law's former teacher, Professor Song. 'Allow me to introduce you to Professor Lin from the Geology Department, who is the leader of this archeological research project,' he said.

Professor Lin nodded and said: 'It's very meaningful for people living in Penghu to come and learn more about the archaeological finds here. These ceramic relics left by our ancestors are worth investigating. In their way, they are— yes, let's say it—priceless.' Professor Lin's voice was very mellow; looking at his face, you would have thought he was chatting and lecturing at the same time. He gestured towards those people carrying sacks behind him. 'This time, we have especially invited these researchers, who work on history and ceramics, in the hope of putting together a more comprehensive research report. I think this will prove very precious.'

'We know too little about the history of Penghu's development. It's such a rare opportunity—I hope the professors and experts here will educate us,' Brother-in-Law said.

'I came to Penghu twice in 1952 on research leave. Here in Jibei, I discovered two sites dating back to the Song

Dynasty and unearthed some Chinese pottery and iron relics, along with some Xining Yuanbao* cash coins made during the reign of Emperor Shenzong in the Northern Song Dynasty. However, it is a pity that the history of pottery and the history of the Song and Yuan Dynasties do not fall within my research area. So I haven't been able to make sense of it all and publish a comprehensive report,' Professor Lin said in his mellow voice. 'Professor Song's participation is very much appreciated. Why are there so many Song and Yuan pottery relics scattered across many of Penghu's isles? With the wisdom and knowledge of these experts, perhaps we will be able to tease out some reason.'

'So these pottery sherds are from the Song and Yuan Dynasties?' I moved closer to Professor Song to take a look at the fragment in his hand. It was difficult indeed to believe that it was seven or eight hundred years old. 'Why are they left on the beach, ignored, unrecognised? Can Penghu trace its development back to so long ago?'

'Good question—this is also a focus of our research,' Professor Song answered.

'Listen, everyone. The experts are here. If you have any questions, wherever possible, please take the opportunity to ask,' Brother-in-Law told us. 'I myself have to seize the opportunity too.'

Lin Bin moved close to me and whispered: 'Perhaps this is merely idle talk, a lie. Penghu is such a desolate place. How can it have a history? Don't be taken in by them—

---

* Coins used between A.D. 1068 and A.D. 1077.

they would think you're a soft target.'

Meanwhile, the kung-fu boy took the lead by raising his hand, asking in a tender, delicate voice: 'The bowls we sell would be returned by our customers if they're chipped, even the tiniest bit chipped. But you've gathered several sacks full of those very things. Where are you going to sell them?'

That group of people with sacks on their backs burst into laughter. Professor Song stroked the boy's head and said: 'Little boy, I told you two days ago—we're not collecting these things to sell them. We're carrying them back to Taipei for research purposes. Do you know what research means?'

'No. Is it a kind of kung-fu?' The boy shook his head, his eyes wide open.

Professor Lin—he whose voice was mellow—scooped the kung-fu boy up into his arms and said to everyone: 'If only my grandson were half as intelligent as he is. If he grows up safe and sound, his inquisitive spirit will contribute hugely to a research career.'

The boy clung to Professor Lin's arms and held onto his neck, apparently not intending to come down for quite some time. Although he was only five or six years old, he didn't look thin. Fearing that Professor Lin might be exhausted, we urged the boy to come down quickly. Out of good will, Ye Ying-San offered to hold him up, but the boy, once again, performed a kung-fu move to scare him, making us all laugh again like drains with the plugs pulled out.

* * *

After dark, we camped on the beach where the big Wooden Fish was given pride of place.

This was real camping. We didn't put up any tents. Rather, we reclined on the coral sand, building only a campfire to boil water. Wang-Xi's aunt brought us a huge pot of rice vermicelli, stir-fried with pumpkins. This was one of Penghu's famous dishes and could be taken as a staple of our diet. Professor Song, Professor Lin, and the other experts probably hadn't tasted it before. And then there were more than ten red tortoise cakes, a huge plate of sea crabs stir-fried with red peppers, and instant-boiled cuttlefish—lugged here in due course by the kung-fu boy in a wicker basket.

The boy didn't want to go home again, insisting on staying with us to do research. Having failed to dissuade him, his mother instructed Wang-Xi: 'I'll leave A-Wen here tonight, please take good care of him. A-Wen rolls around when he sleeps. He falls out of his bed twice every three days. I fear he might tumble into the sea in the middle of the night, and it would be too late to strike the Wooden Fish and the Bronze Bell.'

'It won't happen. I'm with kung-fu,' the boy said, 'and I'll hold onto someone's leg while sleeping.'

'Whose leg do you fancy?' we hurried to ask, somewhat alarmed by his proposal.

'No idea yet. I'll let you know when I've decided.'

The whole pot of pumpkin vermicelli and the fish and crabs in the wicker basket were all consumed. One by one, the stars were emerging, and as each one flickered, it would beckon into view two or three more. This infinity of sky was transformed into a resplendent, magical tableau.

The tranquil sea too was interspersed with star-like fishing lights, which looked as if they were gradually approaching the land, but also as if they were slowly drifting away. I was wondering. On this very sea, seven or eight hundred years ago, had there been so many boats dropping their anchors? Had those people been residents in Jibei or travellers on their way to somewhere else?

The experts of the archaeology team gathered around the campfire. They took out the pottery sherds they had collected, looking carefully at them in the blazing light, and trying to put them together and reconstruct their original shapes. How could these fragments—so broken and loosely scattered—ever be put together? Surely that was unrealistic, wasn't it?

'Such pottery wares were exported from Fujian* in the Song and Yuan Dynasties, fashioned in the styles of Tenmoku bowls and Juko celadon wares,' Professor Song explained.

'Were they exported to Penghu?' I asked.

'According to historical records, there weren't many residents in Penghu during the Song and Yuan Dynasties. They don't seem to have needed so many pottery wares here.'

'Exported to Taiwan?'

'So far, we haven't unearthed any Song and Yuan pottery wares in Taiwan. But in the Philippines, Java, Sumatra, and Malaysia, there have been archaeological finds similar to

---

* A province on the southeast coast of China.

those in Penghu. Their pottery wares are more intact, but their numbers fall far behind the numbers in Penghu. On top of this, such wares are scattered throughout eighteen isles of the Penghu archipelago, including six now uninhabited isles, where there have been abundant finds.'

'This is odd,' Lin Bin said. 'Given that such pottery sherds are all over the coastal areas, and that they were not exported to Penghu, could it be that those people in the Song Dynasty saw Penghu as a dump, where they could throw away their trash?'

'This can't be true!' Ye Ying-San said. 'Could people in the Song Dynasty have had so much leisure time that they sailed so far on their boats, just to dump their rubbish in Penghu? If they had wanted a dump, they could have chosen Quanzhou* instead.'

'I hope you're right. Otherwise, it would be too unfair for us.'

'We've speculated that merchant vessels in the Song and Yuan Dynasties sailed, from Quanzhou, for the countries in the South Sea; they may have regarded Penghu as a way-station or may have come to Penghu to increase and supplement their stock and take shelter. And so they left vast numbers of exported pottery wares here,' Professor Song said.

'Is this sheer speculation?' I asked. 'Or is there any evidence?'

'Good question. What we archaeologists do are precisely these: gleaning information, arranging and summarising,

---

* A large coastal city in Fujian, in southeastern China.

and procuring evidence—only then can we come to a conclusion,' Professor Song said seriously. 'Regarding the development of Taiwan and Penghu in the Song and Yuan Dynasties, historical documents are few and far between, and we haven't been able to locate any record concerning the sea lanes around Penghu. But this doesn't mean these places and these events absolutely did not exist. The pottery sherds we have found and the Song Dynasty sites discovered by Professor Lin may be able to shed light on this forgotten history, providing adequate evidence for us to reach a conclusion after all.'

'Penghu is such an under-developed place. Can it really have a history?' Ye Ying-San asked.

'Is it possible that Penghu's development could have been earlier than that of Taiwan?' Lin Bin asked.

'Why is it that people in Penghu don't know about these things?' I asked.

'Judging from these historical relics, Penghu's first developments were more or less 380 years earlier than Taiwan's,' Professor Lin said. 'Although Penghu served as a portal to Taiwan and was developed fairly early, owing to certain geographical conditions —its small and narrow hinterland, its windy and dry weather, its barren soil, and its sparse population—Penghu's economic development lagged behind. But the fact that Penghu is not prosperous in the economic sense now doesn't mean that we can turn a blind eye to the developments it once underwent—in other words, we shouldn't deny its history.'

'History as we understand it today primarily refers to various sorts of things brought into being by humans, things which are pieced together through time. It embraces a lot of things: politics, economics, military affairs, culture, and other human products—all of these constitute history,' Professor Song said. 'Do you understand what I'm trying to get across? Just because Penghu is not economically prosperous doesn't mean it is void of history.'

'Too difficult. I can't understand,' Lin Bin said.

'But many people tell us that Penghu is under-developed. Even our Geography teacher says so. What can we do?' Ye Ying-San asked. 'Can I have a small pottery sherd, please? Just to show it to our Geography teacher, to give him evidence that there's Song and Yuan Dynasty pottery in Penghu, that Penghu was developed 380 years earlier than Taiwan. I want to see how he will react.'

I placed one sherd in the palm of my hand, gazing upon it.

'Glasses, how will the Geography teacher react when he sees this? What do you think? I reckon he'll quake.'

I shook my head. Perhaps the Geography teacher would throw back his head in laughter, laughing until we were quite out of our depth.

'There'd be no point in that. You need not show it to the Geography teacher,' Brother-in-Law sent forth his voice from a dark corner. He approached us and said: 'The length of history is worth researching in an academic context, but you need not use it to prove that your hometown has a longstanding culture and so stake a claim to a sense of superiority.'

'Why not?' Lin Bin asked.

'History is, after all, history. That's something created

by our ancestors. We didn't take part in its creation. We can be proud of it, certainly, but we can't be so proud as to compare. Comparison in this case would make us lose a sense of our own identities.'

'If we can't compare, we'll definitely lose, won't we?' Ye Ying-San asked. 'And these Song and Yuan pottery wares—what's their relevance to us?'

'Who will always be the loser?' Brother-in-Law grabbed a handful of coral sands and flicked them away, bit after bit, with his thumb. He said: 'Don't regard comparison as a means to put down others and puff up yourself. We should keep our eyes on the present and the future. What's the point of making comparisons if it's only to express a kind of malice? Chen Yi-Xiong asked a good question just now: "Why is it that people in Penghu are not aware of the existence of Song and Yuan pottery?" This means that we have been negligent for too long; we're not paying due attention to our hometown or making sufficient effort to understand it. Now that they've come to our attention, what's truly meaningful about these relics is that, knowing that our ancestors once created a culture and a history here, we will feel even more confident in creating a history of our own that belongs to the present, to our own generation. That is what we should do, rather than using the relics to compare with others, to judge who wins and who loses. This is my opinion. Would you agree?'

'I still feel a little odd. What's wrong with just a bit of comparison?' Ye Ying-San said, picking his ear. Lin Bin scratched his head and said: 'This is unfortunate! We've found something that bears comparison with others at long last, but it turns out that we are not allowed to compare. It's so frustrating.'

Brother-in-Law tapped Lin Bin on the shoulder and said with a smile: 'Once you start making comparisons, there will be no end. Even if Penghu can trace its development back to at least the Song Dynasty in the eleventh century, when we compare ourselves with India, with Egypt, or with Greece, we fall far behind again, do we not?'

'It's not like that,' Lin Bin said. 'According to this logic, when it comes to primitive people, no one can compare with them.'

'If comparison leads to progress, if we don't follow those whose boast is that they "have a longstanding history and culture," but who actually live in a mess, if we compare but only so that we can encourage ourselves to create a new history, then comparison may still be worthwhile.'

The kung-fu boy leant against Wang-Xi, nodding off, as if he thoroughly agreed with Brother-in-Law. In fact, a dribble of saliva was hanging from the corner of his mouth; he was already fast asleep.

Chun-Hua and Chen Xiang-Zhen gathered up the containers and chopsticks and scooped up some seawater to wash them. They talked to each other in low voices and took off their coats to cover the kung-fu boy. 'Can we—on our own—really create a new history?' Chun-Hua asked.

Deep into the night, the sea wind softened; the archaeology team lay down with their clothes on, watching the starry sky and hugging it into their dreams, except for Professor Lin and Professor Song, who, torches in their hands, were still picking at the pottery sherds, inspecting them, comparing them.

'Let's move on and ask a very important practical question,' Lin Bin said to me.

Ye Ying-San and A-Pan followed us, leaving Brother-in-Law sipping sorghum wine alone beside the campfire.

'Professor Song, are you going to glue these sherds together?' Lin Bin asked.

Lin Bin's question shocked me. 'Speak softly.' I knew he wanted to ask how to glue up the broken fretted pen pot.

'We'll try our best. That depends upon the conditions of the broken wares. And the finer they are, the more difficult it is to restore them,' Professor Song said. 'But we need to try our best anyway. If we fail in spite of every effort, then we'll have to give up.'

'Professor Song, what's the best method?' Lin Bin added: 'Please speak softly, Professor Song.'

'Why so secret? Are you afraid of waking everyone up?'

'… Afraid that someone might hear it.'

'In addition to consulting references to find out the original shapes, the key factor is care. And there's this special glue.' Professor Song produced a porcelain vial from his coat-pocket. It was as thin as your index finger, and there was a small stopper on it—very beautifully made, exquisite in its own right. 'Why don't you take this vial? Use it carefully. Don't break it.'

Professor Song's gift was such a surprise that Lin Bin waxed timid, not daring to extend his hand to take it.

'Accept it. Take it as a souvenir. If you see any more ancient relics in Penghu in the future, you can try to glue them together. It will be even more meaningful if local people themselves are willing to engage in such tasks as collecting, categorising, and researching.'

I accepted the porcelain vial on Lin Bin's behalf. Small and exquisite though it was, the vial felt quite heavy when placed on my palm; I hastened to clasp it, fearing that Brother-in-Law might see it and ask us questions. Turning around, I put it in my pocket but could still sense its sagging weight. So I held up my trousers and sat down well away from the campfire.

In the starlight, the tide—wave after wave—was ebbing, rubbing the coral sand into tender sounds, now audible, now faint. I gazed upon the fishing lights—more and more of which were gathering close—and was unable to tell whether they were static or actually sailing towards the sandy coast. In a trance, I imagined they were Song Dynasty merchant vessels—their upper holds storing silk and their lower holds carrying porcelain—and they were approaching the coast to moor up. The people lying sideways by the campfire were Song Dynasty seafarers who had earlier set foot on this coast. Sometimes unfurling, sometimes having to take in their sails, sometimes having to row, shaken and jolted all the way, they were exhausted.

What did people in the Song Dynasty think of the Penghu archipelago? I wondered. An insignificant assemblage of small islands—merely a way-station where they were obliged to come ashore and rest?

Surely there must have been people who had liked this place. Otherwise, how was it that there were people living in Penghu now? Were they descendants of reluctant defending troops called up and forced to station here? Of travellers who had been ill and thus had no alternative but to stay? Surely there must have been people who really appreciated the abundance of fish here, who liked Penghu's fresh water, even if it did taste a bit of salt, and who then decided to settle down here. So I thought.

'Those Song and Yuan Dynasty people who dumped their broken jars and bottles on Penghu's beaches—they really stank,' Lin Bin said. 'You know, the more I think about it, the more furious I am. A way-station is just like a warehouse. Good things are shipped away; rotten, unwanted flawed products are left behind. Everyone remembers pretty things but forgets about the warehouse. Am I being unjust?'

'Stop troubling yourself. Aren't antiques not all in a bit of a state? Some can't even bear a single touch.' Ye Ying-San lay on his back, his hands propped under his head like a pillow. 'Anyway, Penghu's history is 380 years longer than Taiwan's. This is something our Geography teacher cannot deny.'

'Glasses, did you scoff too much pumpkin vermicelli? Why have you been so quiet all night?' Lin Bin asked. 'I know. You're thinking—thinking about your move to Taipei. Penghu is also a way-station for your family, a warehouse for your family, isn't it?'

'A-Bin!' I yelled.

I hadn't imagined Lin Bin would ever utter those words. Moving from Penghu was a matter of the whole family. Even though I didn't want to move, I couldn't have altered my father's decision, could I? True, I was about to leave Penghu, but I still liked this place, still liked my friends and neighbours here. But who would believe me if I said this? Short of breath, I couldn't even speak.

'I'm right beside you. Don't shout. You're waking people up.' Lin Bin asked again: 'Are you thinking then about how to glue up that gift?'

'What gift? Isn't it for gluing up bits of ancient pottery?' Ye Ying-San asked.

A-Pan, who had held his tongue all the while, chose to speak at precisely this moment: 'Our homeroom teacher sent Mr Tao a gift, which was broken by them both, more badly broken than those pottery sherds. They've been troubled by this.'

Lin Bin dragged A-Pan a great distance away: 'Hey, this is a secret! Why are you letting on about it to everyone?'

'Ye Ying-San is one of our gang. He's not anyone.'

'If you let on about it this way, no matter how secret a secret is, it will grow wings and fly all over the place. What should we do if the whole school knows? Such a thing should be kept to ourselves!' Lin Bin, all wired up, admonished A-Pan. 'Now, as a punishment, sing us lullabies, sing until we all fall asleep.'

A-Pan asked us not to look at him. He sat on a ridge of the beach and began to sing, in a tender voice, one song after another. A-Pan had always been an excellent singer. On such a coast, on such a tranquil night—with the sea playing soft melodies in the background and the twinkling stars listening—he cast aside his diffidence and sang his heart out. Even the most careless ear could not have failed to sense the beauty of this voice. A-Pan's only weakness was his being too timid; underlying his polite demeanour was too much bashfulness, too much indecision, which did harm to his singing talent. Such a fine voice, such a serene and beautiful mood—was I to bid them eternal farewell too when moving away from Penghu with my family? This move, did it signify my betrayal of Penghu? I wanted to say, really wanted to say: 'Penghu is not a place I'm passing through in my life. It's forever my hometown.' But on the strength of these few words alone, would Lin Bin have believed me? Would A-Pan, who loved to sing, have believed me? Would Chun-Hua have believed me? Deep in the infinity of the night sky, surely one star at least would have believed me. I too sank into sleep, rapt and wrapt by A-Pan's soft voice.

9

Good endings consist in letting it be

Along the little path leading to the workshop, gaillardias—with their yellow and red hues setting each other off—were in full bloom, huddling together in tufts of three or four, ten or twenty. They grew on the low-lying spots, on the elevated grounds, and at the foot of the Laogu wind-fence; dozens, hundreds, or even thousands of tufts spread out into an immense sea of flowers, confounding the eye.

On our return from the Isle of Jibei, we all became more enthusiastic about pottery making.

Except for Chun-Hua's pair of porcelain pillows, all of us had second or third thoughts about the shapes we wanted. No one gave it utterance, but we all seemed to be pondering the same thing: if the people of the past had not bequeathed to Penghu a single piece of pottery that was unbroken, we at least could make some—something complete and intact—we could do that, couldn't we?

Touch-Me-Not now wanted to make a case decorated with patterns of lotus petals; A-Pan wanted to make a high-necked, bluish white porcelain vase; Lin Bin put aside his plan for the rice vat for the time being, opting instead for a set of patterned bowls and plates—three bowls and six plates, a set of nine. Chen Xiang-Zhen and Ye Ying-San were cooperating to make water jugs and bottles—a set of six, some big, some small.

I was considering changing my work to a narrow-mouthed, wide-shouldered flower vase, a gourd-shaped decanter, or a container in the shape of a seashell for flower arrangement. But having thought it over, again, and then again, I went back to my tea set, my original plan.

'For my tea set, each will have a gaillardia carved into it.'

Having heard this, all the others eagerly followed me in declaring their wish to carve gaillardia petals too. Brother-in-Law smiled and said: 'These shapes require professional skills. Are you quite sure?' We didn't care and didn't want to care.

Immersion in this redesigning process had been so gruelling, making us scratch our heads, and rendering our ears burning hot. None of us could endure yet another change of course, or revision.

But not even these things amounted to the sum of our troubles. What really shocked and upset Lin Bin and me was this: the gift—that broken fretted pen pot—had gone missing.

This had come to our notice the day after our return from Jibei.

Under the wall, there was nothing suspicious; the two pie-like cow pats were still dutifully covering that hole. Even the gaillardia, which Lin Bin had plucked and stuck into the dung, was still there, albeit withered. Why then had the broken pen pot—together with the small blue bag—been taken away? Where and why had they both vanished?

'Strange! To think someone actually wanted those sherds… it's not as if they were age-old antiquities or anything like that.'

Who had taken them away? And for what reason?

Apart from us who attended the pottery workshop, no one else could have known anything about the whole business.

Seven suspects, then. Investigation should be easy enough. Lin Bin and I were of course absolved at once. We assembled the others, and together we all went to the 'scene of crime'.

'It wasn't me, really!' Touch-Me-Not said. Lin Bin and I detected tremors in her voice and immediately fixed our eyes on her in suspicion. She raised that characteristic shoulder of hers, not daring to cast a glance in our direction. 'Really, it wasn't me. I… I am not lying. You can come and search our house,' she added. This was odd. Why had she got that guilty look on her? And she wanted us to search her place!

'Stop being silly, you two. It couldn't have been Wang-

Xi,' Chun-Hua said. 'Since we came back from Jibei, we two have been together all the time. If you suspect her, why don't you suspect me as well?'

'Oh, did the two of you take them away, then?' Lin Bin asked.

'This is so unreal! It was you who broke somebody's gift into pieces, you who dare not admit it, beating about the bush. And now that a cow or something has made off with it, you're pointing the finger at Tom, Dick, and Harry,' Chun-Hua scolded. 'Glasses, don't you collaborate with him… Stupid Lin Bin.'

'You mean neither of you committed the crime,' Lin Bin said. 'Fair enough. Tell me, then, who did take them away.'

'Why are you asking me? Is it any of our business?'

'It wasn't me either. I can swear.' A-Pan spoke for himself before anyone could interrogate him. 'Why don't you check the footprints and see whether it's mine that are there?'

The traces that could serve as forensic evidence had long been obliterated from under our feet. Comparing footprints? How? 'We were too careless. We should have cordoned off the area first!' Lin Bin said, turning his head to glare at Ye Ying-San and Chen Xiang-Zhen.

'Why are you staring at me? It wasn't me. I haven't got any clue about what you lost!'

'You haven't got any clue! Did you not eavesdrop on us in Jibei?'

'Stop using such offensive language. Eavesdrop on what? That gift you were talking about?—I haven't got the least idea what it is, was, should be.'

Everyone was in denial, and there was no one who did not accept the challenge of going to Tianhou Temple to burn incense and take an oath. The pilfering of the small blue bag was declared officially a mystery, resisting and defying any further investigation.

'Could it really be that a cow carried it off?'

That was no more than a flight of fancy, was it? How could that ever have been possible? Which cow was so skilful as to be able to carry off the bag in its mouth and then cover the hole again with those cow pats? That would have been a candidate cow for the Guinness Book of Records: world-beating bovine bag-snatcher!

'Could it be Brother-in-Law himself who had taken the bag away?'

This stood to reason. That day at noon, beside this Laogu wind-fence, he had caught us in the act; his eyes were rolling this way and that—perhaps he caught sight of the small blue bag. But how and why would he have come and excavated it? Out of curiosity? Or perhaps this was the very cloth he had wrapped the fretted pen pot in when presenting it to Sister. Had he carried it back secretly? The pen pot had already been broken anyway—what had he carried it back for?

'That's easy, isn't it? Ask Brother-in-Law! If you don't dare to ask, I'll do it. What do you say?' Chun-Hua said. 'So you'll stop being so deadly suspicious; it hurts our friendship.'

'No way,' I said.

'No way,' Lin Bin joined me.

'If you haven't got the courage, don't ever suspect so-

and-so again from now on,' Chun-Hua said. 'However, I do hope you two can pluck up your courage and admit it to Sister or Brother-in-Law. The pot was broken. So be it. It's not a disaster.'

Chun-Hua flipped her hair and led the gang out of the 'crime scene', leaving Lin Bin and me standing confounded beside the Laogu stonewall. The two of us must have looked like a pair of ham-fisted sleuths who had failed in their mission and now faced the music of all those they had falsely accused. It was much to our chagrin.

'Wu Chun-Hua was right,' Lin Bin said. 'We should confess to Sister that we had broken her gift and lost it too. And that's the long and short of it. Hard cheese!'

Such a thing, how could we confess it? Wouldn't that have made Sister embarrassed? Wouldn't that have twisted the knife in Brother-in-Law's wound? This was out of the question.

'You prefer to be a coward?' Lin Bin asked anxiously, having sensed my unwillingness. 'You'll be laughed at by Chun-Hua and the others for the rest of your life. I swear it!'

* * *

We went through the pottery-making process all over again, and it felt as though it were a brand new start.

One spadeful after another, we set about collecting clay and then carried it back to the workshop for pulverising; we removed the impurities and fetched water to soak and stir the clay. When we began kneading, Brother-in-Law taught us a 'spiral wedging' technique: through twisting and rubbing, the clay was kneaded into the shape of chrysanthemum petals. He said with a smile: 'Kneading clay this way is time-consuming and troublesome, but this is the best way to remove air bubbles from clay, to make it more solid and more dense. As a result of this kneading technique, the clay will become less inclined to crack when we fire it in the kiln.'

In the event, our pottery workshop could have served as a music classroom too.

Lin Bin led the singing. But again and again, A-Pan had to give him a prompt, adding a verse here and a phrase there. Eventually, unable to bear it any longer, he simply took over the lead.

Ye Ying-San's whistling, though not too impressive to begin with, ended up not being too cacophonous—and it was quite pleasant to the ear too—after repeated practice, in accompaniment of our singing. This greatly boosted our confidence. Even Touch-Me-Not was humming away, and never mind everybody else.

Compared with the kneading and the moulding of the raw clay, trimming and decorating pottery wares demanded much more care: using bamboo knives to scratch and scrape; smoothing the edges with soft leather; sponges, rolling pins, paddles, abrasive files, fringe-shaped brushes, toothed ribs, and a tool resembling a bamboo-copter, small and rather lovely, which served to measure the diameter and depth of a pottery ware—looking at these tools alone would dazzle you, and that's before you even begin to try to use them, before your hands—fuddled and confounded—are all fingers and no thumbs.

'It's so hard to get used to them! I can't shake off the feeling that actually they're really unhandy,' I said.

'It's because we're not adept yet. But this doesn't mean they're clumsy, cumbersome.' Brother-in-Law smiled, clapped, and resumed: 'Let's smooth off those angles and edges! When the wares go into the kiln, we don't want them to hit one another; we don't want them all damaged.'

Brother-in-Law was busy at a separate workbench, sculpting a clay bottle, again and again, with a thin and sharp bamboo strip. What was that shape? My heart shuddered—what was he making?

With his head lowered, Brother-in-Law gouged a mesh-like opening out of the clay bottle with meticulous care. He was so slow that his movements appeared to be frozen. I stopped my work to stare at that clay bottle. There, carved on the clay body were thin lines crisscrossing each other— the whole the spitting image of a fretted pen pot. I couldn't be wrong: Brother-in-Law was making a new pen pot. He was sculpting it stroke after stroke.

Brother-in-Law took a deep breath and slowly exhaled, nodding towards me. He appeared to be addressing me but also seemed to be talking to himself: 'Best let it be. Being too pernickety, pressing too hard, can hinder rather than help the outcome.' He gouged out yet another mesh-like opening with the bamboo strip and added: 'It's broken; so it is. Can't be put together. Why not make another one, in memory of it?'

Brother-in-Law's words went un-noticed by the others, who were all engrossed with their own pottery wares.

When I come to think about it, I was the only one who actually registered what he had said.

And that was the moment at which the whole business about the fretted pen pot was resolved, almost resolved, that is: it was a secret to be kept by only Brother-in-Law and me, and there was no need for further questions. The only thing that still confused me was his injunction 'don't press too hard', insofar as it touched upon his relationship with Sister. What on earth was it that was not going well between them? They seemed to suit each other so perfectly; what was keeping them apart? I didn't understand these things, and it wasn't for me to intrude. Even if I had known what the situation really was, I wouldn't have had enough confidence to succeed in cheering him up. This matter… I could only leave it alone perhaps.

Brother-in-Law rubbed his forehead and smiled bitterly. All of a sudden, he cried out: the thin, sharp bamboo strip he was holding had knifed into the corner of his right eyebrow. Blood was gushing out.

'Are you okay? Are you okay?'

The area around his eye and eyebrow was at once covered in blood. We were tossed into chaos, some rushing to find the first-aid kit, others drawing out handkerchiefs, and all of us milling around Brother-in-Law. A-Pan produced his handkerchief but was afraid to move forward, asking: 'Has the eye been poked out? Ah!'

'I'm fine. Don't worry.' Brother-in-Law took out his own handkerchief and pressed it on the corner of his eyebrow. 'I was absent-minded. The pain will pass. No worries. The pain will pass…' He lifted his handkerchief and showed us his wound.

Near the tip of his eyebrow was a wound of almost one inch long. The blood had been staunched, but there was a transparent fluid seeping out and trickling down his cheek.

'Amitabha! Sir, you almost became one-eyed.' Chun-Hua brought the first-aid kit, wanting to put some ointment on Brother-in-Law's wound. 'Thank heavens you're alright, but the wound must be very painful.'

'I'm healthy. All of my wounds mend very quickly.' Brother-in-Law looked at us in embarrassment and said: 'Many apologies for the alarm. I appreciate your care. Please don't worry. I'll be fine.'

That thin, sharp bamboo strip which was to blame was stained with Brother-in-Law's blood. Instead of cleaning it, he deftly slipped the strip around the mouth of the newly made pen pot. The blood was quickly absorbed into the clay, as if a dark brown glaze had been applied to it. He carried on sculpting the pen pot, meticulously trimming those openings, one by one, into heart shapes. This was indeed a labour of love, a work of his heart and blood. I wondered who would receive it in the future.

And would that person cherish it? Entrusting my own wishes to an unknowable future, was I being too whimsical?

10

Magical changes in the kiln

Chun-Hua was the first to be told that I was definitely leaving Penghu. My father had come back from Taipei. He said the coral business had settled into a steady state of growth, and he had come back specifically to transfer me to the new school. The day on which we were to move had also been settled: the twenty-third of July, or the seventeenth of the sixth month in the Lunar Calendar, which is the day of the Great Heat.

One day, on the little path leading to the workshop, I told Chun-Hua about the news. Hearing it, she uttered a single 'oh' and carried on walking, walking faster and faster until, unexpectedly, she began to dash forward, dashing up a hillside that was abloom with gaillardias.

Chun-Hua squatted and cupped a bouquet of gaillardias in her hands, asking me in a loaded voice: 'Chen Yi-Xiong, you are really glad about it, aren't you?'

'No. My dad said it was inauspicious to move during the seventh month in the Lunar Calendar, so we're moving earlier.'

'Chen Yi-Xiong, don't you like going to Taipei?' Chun-Hua had softened her voice.

'Taipei is where it's all happening, but I'll tell them, I'll say I'm from Penghu.'

'Really? Dare you tell this to your classmates in Taipei?' she asked softly and slowly.

'I dare.'

'Dare you say that again and again? Not afraid your classmates may laugh at you?' She rose to her feet, but her eyes were still rested on the gaillardias blooming all over the place.

'I dare to say it. That's all. Why do I have to say it more than once?' I raised the pitch of my voice and went on: 'What's there to laugh about? Penghu was developed 380 years earlier than Taiwan!' I clenched my fists but had no idea whom I was angry with, only feeling a heat spreading through my body, as if my feet were off the ground, powerless. I couldn't even stand steady—I was so angry.

Chun-Hua wouldn't look me in the face. 'Will you remember us, remember these people? Will I be the first to be forgotten?' she asked slowly, as before.

'Please don't keep asking these questions.' How should I put it? 'I won't forget you… any of you. Don't you believe me?'

I felt as if my heart were trussed up by a twisted coil of rope; every question of hers exerted a tightening force—and the grip was agonising. I was in no position to know what it would be like after moving to Taipei, after transferring to the new school, and I couldn't tell now what would be the best things to say and to do if I were to get off to a good start with my new classmates. How would they see me?

Although I loved my birthplace Penghu, I also looked forward to Taipei's hustle and bustle. These two places—I liked them both. Was this necessarily a contradiction? In liking both, was I really betraying Penghu?

'Would you like me to tell everyone that, in just ten days, you're leaving?'

'Later please. Let me think about how best to break it to them.' I too squatted and then sat down properly. That way I could see Chun-Hua. She was crying.

* * *

The clay wares, which had been given their finishing touches, stood in a row in a shaded place outside the workshop to dry, covered with wet cloth, with newspapers beneath them. It was a cameo of us actually, of Brother-in-Law and us sitting in a row, keeping cool, and chatting.

'We want our clay wares to dry evenly. Those works that are especially thick need to be covered with wet cloth lest their surfaces should dry up too rapidly, in which case the amounts of moisture inside and outside would be uneven, and they would crack in the kiln,' Brother-in-Law said.

'We could dry the clay wares straightaway in sunlight, but it's better to wait until their moisture content is lower, until gradually it has evaporated, and then to put them into the sun.'

'How long will that take? I want to dry them in the sun straightaway,' Lin Bin said.

'Sure. Of course you can try!' Brother-in-Law was speaking fast and clearly but with a smile. But this made Lin Bin pause before he turned his head to ask us: 'Is anyone up for joining me and drying their wares in the sun?'

The row of us sitting by the wall gave no response.

'You're all cowards. Scared, aren't you? Watch me.' Lin Bin carried that set of patterned bowls and plates he had moulded, one by one, into sunlight: three bowls and six plates, arranged into three files. Less than ten minutes later, our very own Mr Lin began to scratch his head, press his ear, and glance here and there; and then he began to carry his works back in, one by one, leaving only a small bowl on the edge of the shade. 'You think I'm a laughing stock? No, no, no! Out of the question. But I'll leave only one work for experiment purposes, you see. What? You don't even dare.'

With this, Lin Bin's one-man show came to a standstill, a hasty close.

Chen Xiang-Zhen rose suddenly. 'Sir, when will our works be fired and finished? In how many days?' she asked Brother-in-Law, but her eyes were fixed on me.

'There are some remaining steps: biscuit firing and glazing—only after these can we proceed to glaze firing.

Firing in the kiln alone takes three days and three nights, and the fire must burn continuously.'

'Will we make it in time?' Chun-Hua murmured.

Together, we pushed the oil drum to the vicinity of the kiln and, without delay, carried our clay wares over with both hands. A-Pan was trailing behind Brother-in-Law, muttering: '… Recently I've been thinking about the same question everyday: I don't know what to do when I grow up.'

'Do you know what your talents and interests are?' We crowded before the entrance to the kiln, wanting to put our clay wares inside. Brother-in-Law held us back with one arm. 'We need a plan before filling the kiln: observe the kiln first and decide on an order. Otherwise, it won't accommodate all that many wares, and we won't be able to stow them properly.'

'Everyone says I'm a good singer. I'd like to study vocal music.'

'But what do you think? Other people praise you—that's all very well. But you have to judge and come to your own conclusion.'

Brother-in-Law asked A-Pan to carry all the clay wares, one by one, into the kiln. 'Put the bigger ones inside first,' he said, 'and lodge the smaller ones in between them. You can stack them on top of each other, but be careful not to crush the wares underneath.' And then he added: 'It's very nice of course to settle early on a goal for life, but why not leave some space for your other talents? After all, there's still a long way to go.'

After the oil supply pipe had been filled with the heavy

crude oil, Brother-in-Law lit a fire; together, A-Pan and I shut the kiln. Immediately, through the observation port, we saw flames blazing. Brother-in-Law hastened to adjust the oil control valve. 'In the beginning of the firing process, the fire can't be too strong. There's still moisture in the clay wares. If the temperature rises too rapidly, the wares will burst… Okay, it's enough for today. Who can stay and keep watch over the fire?'

Ye Ying-San's pigs were having diarrhoea again; with an armful of white popinac leaves and twigs, he had to go home first. Others left one after another, leaving just me to watch over the kiln fire with A-Pan.

We sat at the entrance to the kiln. A-Pan rested his chin on his knees, facing the kiln, lost in profound thought.

'A-Pan, I think your voice is a good one. You'll do well in the future if you study singing.'

'That… perhaps.' But his eyes and facial expression exuded a confidence that seemed unfamiliar to me. 'I fear only that my parents can't afford it,' he added.

The heat from the kiln was so intense that I moved a few inches backward. 'A-Pan, I… my family is moving.'

'I know, on the twenty-third of July.' With his head rested on his knees, A-Pan did not budge an inch. Taken aback, I moved further away. 'Did Wu Chun-Hua tell you that?'

'My dad heard it at the Fishermen's Association. What's more, your family is eventually emigrating to Canada.'

I was so shocked that I gasped, coughing abruptly and fiercely. 'Why wasn't I told?' I exclaimed in a hoarse voice.

'Perhaps you were the only person in Magong who

didn't know it.'

'Do Ye Ying-San and the others know it?'

A-Pan turned his head, his eyes riveted on me. To my consternation, he nodded.

I took to my heels and ran, yelling in my heart: 'Why wasn't I told?' I was about to become a foreigner, a stranger to my friends, and everyone in Magong had known this, everyone except for me! Why were they all hiding it from me? Were they all laughing at me behind my back? I ran for it.

I ran in great strides through the white popinacs and onto the little path.

Wu Chun-Hua and Touch-Me-Not were walking side by side some distance in front of me. Apparently they heard my steps and turned their heads to look.

I overtook them, dashing past them without halting.

'Glasses, what happened to you?' Chun-Hua shouted. 'You wouldn't need to run so fast if you were chased by a cow! Yi-Xiong, what happened?'

Still running, I arrived at the gap in the Laogu stonewall and saw that the passage was blocked by that bullock again. Lin Bin was painstakingly climbing the wall; he had just reached the top. I made a jump for it and pulled one leg after the other across the bullock's back. I heard Lin Bin cry out—'Wow!'—from the top of the wall: 'Glasses! Why are you so brave today?' He turned over and jumped down from the wall, trailing after me. 'Have you fallen out with Wu Chun-Hua and others?'

I ignored him, supported my glasses with one hand, and dashed on. Passing through the campus, I collided with Ye Ying-San and Chen Xiang-Zhen. In the distance, Lin Bin yelled and shouted: 'Stop him! Stop Glasses! He's gone stark raving mad!'

Ye Ying-San handed over that armful of white popinac leaves and twigs to Chen Xiang-Zhen and spread out his arms to stop me.

Right or left, I couldn't get past him. Grabbed by Ye Ying-San by the waist, I struggled hard. And both of us fell onto the ground. 'Glasses, Glasses! What's the matter? Running so fast! Your face is as white as a sheet!' He supported me to my feet and gripped my shoulder, asking again: 'The sun is glaring hot. Running like this, you'd scare everyone in Magong to death. What on earth is going on?'

I was gasping desperately for air but couldn't manage to gulp down even the half of what I needed.

Running after me, Wu Chun-Hua and the others caught up too. Lin Bin pressed his waist with a hand and said: 'You didn't have to run so fast even if you were desperate for the toilet. Look at him! He can't even blow out a candlewick now! There was no fire, there was no shipwreck, and no one was chasing him, but he was dashing like a mad cow! Blimey. Thanks to you, my stomach hurts.'

'My family is leaving for Taipei. And then for Canada.' I was still out of breath.

They all stared at me blankly. 'Just for that, you were running like mad? Were you making a dash to Canada already? Peanuts! Don't scare us like that, Glasses,' Lin Bin said.

Chun-Hua grasped my elbow and passed me her handkerchief: 'Amitabha! You look all done in after the race. Wipe yourself a bit!' And she said to all of us: 'Come on. Walk slowly. No one's running any more. Let's go and rest our legs at the Guanyin Pavilion.'

We came to the Guanyin Pavilion and sat ourselves down in a row on the stone steps in the front.

On the beach, where the tide was rising, those stone weirs—used to trap fish and stacked into lovely patterns— were all submerged from sight. The tide was rising noiselessly. Wherever our eyes roamed, everything out there was calm and serene.

Only the wind, in the back of my head, was still blowing, slowly blowing.

I spotted a single red fiddler crab with its two claws raised, one bigger than the other. Moving by fits and starts, the crab was making its way towards where we were sitting. It set me thinking: perhaps its cave had been lashed by the sea and, unable to stay any longer, it had ventured out and crawled all the way in order to take refuge here on the square. But was it in flight or was it just enjoying itself? The crab seemed to have noticed us—it stopped short, afraid to move.

Lin Bin rose to his feet and said: 'A souvenir for Glasses. I'll capture it. Why not let him take it away?' No sooner had he descended the stone steps than the red fiddler crab turned and ran, fleeing for all it was worth in the direction of that stone tablet, the one inscribed with the Chinese characters 石敢當*.

Chun-Hua stopped Lin Bin: 'Don't mess around with it!

---

* 石敢當 (Shigandang), erected to ward off evil spirits.

Leave it alone! Don't you see it's terrified? Do you think a crab would have strayed all the way up here on a whim? This one must have been forced to do so.'

There were clearly many things on my mind I wanted to find words for, but they were all tangled up—I couldn't settle on what to say first, and being pent up like that was painful. I got to my feet. They were all alarmed. Lin Bin called out to Ye Ying-San immediately, and both made a move to grab me. 'I've barely come to myself after all that frenzy of running. What now? You're hell bent on making us chase you again?'

'Tomorrow, I'll bring my camera. We'll take a picture together, with Brother-in-Law,' I said. 'Would you be so kind as to have a picture taken with me?'

'Chen Yi-Xiong, don't say that. How could you say that!?' someone muttered these words, reducing all of us to silence. And in that mood of quietus, we stayed where we were, still sitting there when the sun sank below the sea. I felt as if I were still trying to catch my breath. Try as I did, I couldn't manage to breathe deeply, breathe in, breathe out. My brain was teeming with rumbling noises.

* * *

It took one day and one night for the biscuit-fired wares to cool off completely.

Chun-Hua's pair of pillows and Touch-Me-Not's lotus-petalled case came out intact. Ye Ying-San's water bottles and one of Lin Bin's patterned bowls had cracked, looking now like gearwheels, toothy. No surprise there, sadly; this was the product of Lin Bin's experimental exposure to strong sunlight.

Brother-in-Law's pair of fretted pen pots and my tea set were covered with a layer of white ash. I dusted them off with a fine-haired brush; to my relief, they were intact too.

The clay wares that had been biscuit-fired were almost finished. Lying there in our hands, they appeared solid and plain and boasted a charm of their own—looking good even though still unglazed.

The glaze vials were labelled one after another with beautiful names: Yellow Seto, Candy, Persimmon, Tenmoku, Green Tapestry, Cinnabar, Liuli Glass, and Dark Eye. These vials—whose colours didn't seem significantly different, one from another—could they really metamorphose into such a variety of hues?

'From applying glazes to firing in the kiln for the second time, it's a magical process: with two percent of ferric oxide, the transparent glaze will turn into a translucent glaze of yellowish brown; the slightest variation in the amount triggers a change in the colour. You can even transform bright beige into black,' Brother-in-Law said. 'The changes in the kiln often exceed all your expectations; some say this is part of the great fun of ceramic art.'

'If it's so uncontrollable, we may as well smear the glazes at random,' Lin Bin said.

'Being fired in the kiln, the colours on the clay wares will undergo changes, but as long as we exercise strict control from the outset, even if the results do not turn out as expected, they won't stray too far from our wishes—at least beige won't turn into black once it has been fired,'

Brother-in-Law said. 'We need to prepare ourselves for accidents, but we can't go back on our initial plans and endeavours.'

Holding the wares in our hands, we each went in search of the glazes we liked and set about painting or drizzling the glazes according to our intentions. Brother-in-Law sat in the low chair near the front entrance, carefully cleaning his pair of fretted pen pots. Seeing me approach, he lifted the pen pot in his hand and said: 'No matter how its colour will change, its original shape will remain the same.' Then he laughed heartily, rubbing that scar near the tip of his eyebrow with the back of his hand. 'Chen Yi-Xiong, be it Taipei or Canada, try to like the place. As long as you never quite lose sight of your hometown in the back of your mind, one day, when you're in a position to do so, you'll do something for this place. Rest assured and go for it.'

I ruminated and wanted to say 'I'll bear this in mind'. But nothing was said; I only nodded, lodging those words of encouragement deep in my heart.

We carried our glazed wares one by one back into the kiln and ignited the oil to fire them. Camera raised, I kept taking snapshots.

Chun-Hua led Touch-Me-Not and Chen Xiang-Zhen to dye sheets of mian paper* into various colours. Touch-Me-Not dexterously folded the paper into a big flower ball, and Ye Ying-San climbed onto the workbench to hang it

---

* A kind of paper used for calligraphy and painting in East Asia; so-called 'cotton paper'.

up there in the centre.

Grasping a handful of those cascading, colourful ribbons of paper, Lin Bin laughed and laughed. 'Please remember this for me. When I get married, I want the wedding hall decorated like this,' he told A-Pan.

To our surprise, A-Pan said: 'Okay. Same here.'

With all this laughter, the three girls slumped into a heap. The big flower ball suspended under the skylight started slowly to go round and round. 'A-Pan, you concentrate on your singing. Never imitate him,' Chun-Hua said, laughing again.

Amidst of all this hilarity, we managed to take a group photo, one which preserved our brightest smiles in perpetuity.

We proposed to invite Sister to our farewell party. Brother-in-Law agreed, and he was going to invite her himself.

It was the fifteenth of the sixth month in the Lunar Calendar: the moon that night was every bit the match for the one on the night of the Mid-Autumn Festival.

We opened the kiln and retrieved our pottery works. Holding the glossy and sparkling wares in our hands, we looked at them and eagerly displayed them to the other admiring eyes. Ye Ying-San carried his water jugs to us, crying out: 'Look! Aren't they beautiful?' He smiled from ear to ear and capered around the workshop in circles with those jugs in his hands, almost bumping into Lin Bin's set of patterned bowls.

In such a jocund mood, the farewell party thrown for me and the ceremony of bringing our pottery lessons to a close were in full swing—and this did much to soothe my heart. A farewell party should be exactly like this, full of cheerful good wishes, shouldn't it? It was a pity that, in the end, Sister did not turn up at our party. She would never have realised the degree to which the pottery lessons had changed our temperaments, would never have known how sorry we had been for her and Brother-in-Law; she didn't know we had promised to come back for a reunion twenty years on, never knowing how keenly we had hoped she would come.

Towards the end of the party that day, Brother-in-Law called all of us back to the workshop. On the workbench, he spread out a sheet of mian paper, each end of which was held down with one of that pair of flawless pen pots, the ones which had just come out of the kiln. With his wrist suspended in the air—and with unruffled calm—he wielded his brush, writing out a line of Chinese characters in beautiful semi-cursive script: 努力愛春華—cherish well your youthful days.

'It's for Chen Yi-Xiong, isn't it?' Lin Bin laughed uproariously, making eyes at me, for the Chinese phrase for 'youthful days' is identical to Chun-Hua's written name. 'I knew it. I knew it!'

But Brother-in-Law went on to slice another sheet of mian paper, writing out the same line on it: 努力愛春華. 'One for each of you. Once gone, our youthful days will never come back. Think more, learn more, feel more, and cherish this stage of your life.'

Gazing upon those Chinese characters, which were impregnated with rich black ink, I gently smoothened the creased corners of the paper. The fragrance of ink reminded me of the scent of gaillardias in the sun, which seeped into our lungs and refreshed every inch of our bodies.

Outside the pottery workshop, gaillardias were just at their best. That window in the workshop resembled the frame of a painting: in the foreground, gaillardias blooming all over the place and dancing in the breeze; in the middle ground, one after another of that deep dark Laogu wind-fences; three cows appearing, swinging their tails, and ambling through the midst of the flowers and the stonewalls. At the far end of the landscape, beneath the horizon, lay the aquamarine belt of sea; on the sea were colourful fishing boats—three or four of them—and the waves, rolling up and breaking at their sterns, fanned out, the foam mixing with the water and mirroring the beauty of those few white clouds in the blue sky.

What I saw at that moment was also a page in the book of my youthful days. From that moment on, the tableau, the never-to-fade tableau, would be forever etched into the journal of my life, wouldn't it?

11

Wearing the medal of homecoming

The sky is darkening; the glow of the setting sun is tranquil and still, but it also resembles the first blush of dawn. The northeast wind carries moisture; I imagine it, too, as morning dews, which ever so slightly moisten my clothes. Yes, that's the mood I'm in: that light in the pottery workshop, which has just been turned on, looks as if it were a sun newly emerged from the sea, so soft and warm—if there isn't a magnetic force hidden in its radiance, how is it that I'm walking faster and faster like this? Carrying the basket of red mangos in one hand, why do I feel as if I were being pulled by something, with my legs escaping my control and moving on faster and faster?

In front of the workshop, a blaze of light bursts into my eyes; its smoke, opalescent in colour, is rising into the sky, in wreaths that are growing increasingly dense. That crisp laughter, heard from the distance, brings to mind the tintinnabulation of cowbells reverberating across a grass-grown hillside. Who, having arrived so early, has lit up the bonfire? Yes, it can only be they. It's been twenty years, my old friends.

I stop beside the Laogu stonewall to wipe my glasses; and I thrust my chest out, making my way to the pottery workshop in wide but tentative strides, as though this were my first time coming here.

I slow down and softly slip to the back of the pottery workshop. Passing through the tuft of white popinacs, I suddenly realise that those people around the bonfire are a knot of thirteen or fourteen-year-old boys and girls. 'Ah!' I cry out and halt. How can it be that these are young people? How can they be the ghosts of our youthful selves? I'm almost aghast.

Noticing my approach, they smile shyly. The boys rub their hands and brush off the dirt. The girls pinch the creases of their long skirts, staring at me with their chins tucked in.

'Excuse me, are you…?'

'We're all taking pottery lessons here, just like you,' a boy of a strong build and with thick, curly hair says. 'May I ask whether you are Uncle Chen Yi-Xiong? You're the fourth. Three others have arrived. They're talking in the workshop.'

I stare at him, surprised. Something about the boy's

features strikes me as familiar. If he were not so much younger than I am, I would wager I'd seen him somewhere. Yes, I *have* seen him.

'I knew it all along. Is that you wearing glasses in the photo on the display shelf? It's you, isn't it?' Hearing these words, the girls huddle together and chuckle. I make a move for the workshop, only to be stopped by him again: 'Thanks for coming. The band will play you into the workshop.'

'You look so much like someone. But I can't remember who or where I've seen the person before,' I tell the curly-haired boy, smiling.

'Me? I look like my dad.'

One and all, the children burst into uproarious laughter. 'Who can match you for naughtiness?'

'His name is Tao Yi-De. His dad is our teacher,' a girl with beautiful teeth says. 'Of the seven of us, he's the most mischievous. Am I right?'

'You're Mr Tao's son?'

'Yes, he is. He wants us to call him Senior. Nobody cares a fig for it!' the girl says.

'Glasses!' someone calls out from behind me.

That person walking out of the workshop—just a single glance and I know exactly who he is. Ye Ying-San!

He gives me a punch in the chest, making me stumble backward. Straightaway, the woman standing beside him makes a lunge to stop me falling. 'You're old enough now to wean yourself from such boyish behaviour. Oh dear! The children are all watching closely, Councillor Ye!' the woman scolds, glaring at him. Now she turns her head and yells: 'Chen Xiang-Zhen, take your husband back and give him some discipline.'

What! So it's real? Ye Ying-San really married Chen Xiang-Zhen? I goggle at them and turn to look attentively at the woman who was speaking. She behaves naturally and confidently, extremely charming and graceful in manner. But she can't be Chun-Hua.

'Mr Class Leader, you're so bad at recognising people. You don't know who I am? I—yes, the very person in front of you—I am Lin Wang-Xi.'

'Touch-Me-Not? Are you really Touch-Me-Not?'

'You've got it. I most certainly am,' she says loudly. 'Don't call me Touch-Me-Not any more. Now, I can't manage to put on a shy look even if I want to.' She dissolves into laughter, looking for all the world like a paeony in full bloom.

Standing at the entrance to the workshop, isn't that person Brother-in-Law? He's still wearing that bristly, bedraggled hair, that cotton shirt, and that black pair of kung-fu shoes, and there's his trademark—that bitter smile.

'Chen Yi-Xiong, I knew for sure you would come back. Welcome.'

I step forward, hold out my hand, and the memory of Brother-in-Law's strong grip suddenly comes back to me. I want to pull my hand back, but it's too late. It feels as though my hand were pinched by a closing door. 'Ouch!' I cry out.

Ye Ying-San claps and laughs out loud, saying: 'Same as before. Mr Tao's vice-like grip is just as firm and strong as ever, isn't it? Glasses, how could you forget even this?'

'Come on in. We made a pot of tea just now—it's getting cold,' Touch-Me-Not calls out at the top of her voice. 'Coming back from so far away, you must be very thirsty. Come in and take a seat. We'll talk the hind legs off a donkey.'

There hasn't been much change in the interior of the workshop. The long workbench is still situated in the middle. The mesh screens, water ladles, and water pipes are irregularly positioned along the wall, just as they once were. Our group photo has been enlarged and framed, standing there upon the display shelf, accompanied by a profusion of ceramic wares. Those young and timid smiling faces invite my perusal; I can't draw my eyes away. But Touch-Me-Not pulls me away: 'Stop looking. It makes you feel old. Come. Sit down. We heard you'd got a doctorate and had become a professor. Is this true?'

'We'll talk about this later. Before that, let me know how you've been, okay?'

'Me? Everyday, I stir-fry chillies and cover myself in fumes from morning to night, selling two hundred meals. I've turned into an unlovely old woman. There's nothing to talk about in that, is there?' she says, laughing.

Had I come across Touch-Me-Not in the streets of Magong, surely I wouldn't have recognised her by any means. Such a lively presence, so cheerful and so full of confidence—how can that be the same person as the Touch-Me-Not we once knew, the Touch-Me-Not who used to raise a shoulder and tilt her head, who could be shocked into tears at the drop of a hat.

'More about me? I got married at twenty-one—mother of three now, the oldest in his fourth grade this year. My husband is the most honest man in Penghu. He's even afraid of letting me know it when he wants to go angling on his days off,' Touch-Me-Not says sonorously and laughs sonorously too. 'Good heavens! What has made me become so terrifying?'

'We got married on Ye Ying-San's return from his national service. His mother had asked me to take care of him. Who would have guessed this was a commitment for life?' Xiang-Zhen is wearing her dark and sleek hair in a bun. Her speech and manner too exude a mature feminine charm. 'He studied marine engineering at the fishery vocational school here and spent five years at sea. After that, he worked for the Fishermen's Association, until he was elected a County Councillor.' She and Ye Ying-San are sitting next to each other. The more I look at them, the more their faces seem to match each other. With his arms folded and rested on the workbench, Ye Ying-San smiles but doesn't say a word, quietly listening instead to Xiang-Zhen talking, his face a pattern of felicity and contentment.

'He has been re-elected twice. Every time it was he who got the most votes,' Touch-Me-Not says. 'I was Ye Ying-San's volunteer campaigner. Each time I had to wear out three pairs of sneakers and had to rush about until I got cramps in both legs. You haven't seen it, but from the lectern, he can really hit the mark. To be honest, of all the County Councillors in Penghu, he's the most outspoken, the best orator!'

How could I not know this? Twenty years ago, it was I who had personally borne the brunt of his policy declarations delivered from a wooden fish crate.

'He has many opinions. Instead of complaining about this and that to me everyday, it does him good to go into the world and put his ideas into practice. And I can enjoy some peace and quiet too,' Chen Xiang-Zhen says.

'How many children have you got?' I ask. 'Why didn't you bring them over? I'd love to meet them.'

'They're as naughty as can be. The last time we went to the cafeteria, the three of them made enemies of Touch-Me-Not's three darlings, and they got into a fierce fight. The customers were all frightened off.' Chen Xiang-Zhen asks me: 'Our Mr Driver will come, will he not?'

'It was he who went to the port to pick me up today. He should be here soon. What about A-Pan and Chun-Hua?'

'A-Pan rang and told me he hadn't forgotten today's reunion, but he's going to meet us on television,' Ye Ying-San says. 'On tonight's Mid-Autumn Festival special programme, he'll sing us a song. Did you know he has become a very popular singer?'

Tao Yi-De, the curly-haired boy, comes to us in a rush, saying: 'We've burned up nearly all the firewood.' Behind him was that girl with beautiful teeth, poking her head out to look at us, and saying with a sweet smile: 'The moon has come out.'

We walk out of the workshop. 'Where's Chun-Hua? Is she still in Penghu? She hasn't left, has she?' I ask Ye Ying-San.

'Didn't Lin Bin tell you?'

'What happened to her?' I shake my head. Seeing Ye Ying-San's strange look, I begin to feel nervous. I turn to Chen Xiang-Zhen and Touch-Me-Not, but they ask me the same question: 'Didn't Lin Bin tell you?'

'Is she not coming tonight?'

'I'm not sure. Chun-Hua is a person who cherishes all relationships. I can't think that she would have forgotten our reunion. Even if she has renounced the world, can this friendship ever be consigned to oblivion?' Touch-Me-Not says. 'It's been ten years since she became a Buddhist nun at Fo Guang Shan*.'

I feel as if someone had punched me hard in my head; my eyes are blinded by white flashes! Touch-Me-Not takes me to the tuft of horsetail trees, and Chen Xiang-Zhen follows us.

'Glasses, don't be sad,' Chen Xiang-Zhen says. 'This was her own choice. She must have thought it through very carefully. You mustn't see her in the light of worldly values, Glasses. We work hard for our daily living, and she for what she believes. She's living a very peaceful life. Ying-San and I visited her once at Fo Guang Shan. Her dharma name is Ci-Ming.'

'Why did she do this?'

'Glasses, it's not for us to feel sad for her,' Chen Xiang-Zhen resumes. 'If you really want to know why, spare some time and visit her at Fo Guang Shan. But I'd advise you to think it over first. Ying-San and I, seeing her so peaceful and resolute, could only put our palms together and wish

---

* A large Buddhist monastery located in Kaohsiung, Taiwan.

her all the best. If you go there just to ask her questions, you'll only disturb her monastic life. And Ci-Ming may not necessarily be willing to answer you, I think. Glasses, respect her choice. Wish her well.'

All of a sudden, a flurry of rockets shoots up from the bonfire, and instantly they are transformed into a dazzle of flames. Whoosh! Whoosh! They shoot up into the night sky. Looking up, I see the moon hanging high between the twigs of the horsetail trees.

The curly-haired boy Tao Yi-De yells: 'Beautiful! Beautiful! Encore!'

Encore? Long ago I too seem to have yelled just like that.

Yes, when we were on our way to the pottery workshop for the first time, Chun-Hua left the rest of us behind and leapt over the Laogu wind-fence all by herself—her agile movement, back then, drew the same yell from me. In no way can I believe that black hair of hers, so beautifully combed, has all been shaven off. In no way can I embrace the image of her agile body dressed in a kasaya robe, walking in solemn piety with her palms joined together.

In the middle of their merrymaking, the children hurry to get themselves into the right positions, whispering to each other: 'Coming, coming, another person's coming. Get the band ready.'

They pick up the pots and plates on the ground, striking them as improvised percussion instruments. Their humming voices—because they can only just suppress the urge to laugh—are all out of tune.

As expected, the person emerging from the dark is the

Thin Boy Lin Bin. With his beer belly bulging, he says: 'What kind of band is this? Let's have it again. And look! Look whom I've brought with me!'

Whom could Lin Bin have invited? Who's coming with him?

The children re-formed themselves. It looks as if they want to pound out some proper music this time, but they still can't hold back their laughter: their voices are still out of tune. We all crane our necks and direct our eyes towards the white popinacs. Someone is indeed moving towards us, slowly and softly moving towards us.

Before anyone can react, the girl with the beautiful teeth breaks away from the band, running and exclaiming: 'Mum, why are you here as well?'

Sister! The person walking towards us is none other than Sister, our homeroom teacher.

Apart from Brother-in-Law, who remains fixed, all of us swarm forward, shouting in unison: 'Madam, Madam!' We've already entered middle age, but evidently we haven't learned how to restrain ourselves. Chen Xiang-Zhen and Touch-Me-Not, each holding one of Sister's hands, say in sweet voices: 'Madam, you really should come.'

Married, they now have their own families, each and every one. In retrospect, twenty years' time seems but a transient moment—all you have to show for it is a fleeting glance. Yet when I contemplate the passage of time and see its evidence in front of me, I find everywhere the signs of time's fickleness, something which no one could ever have predicted with certainty. Sister and Brother-in-Law, married to different people, have their own children now.

Sister heaves a sigh of relief and says with a smile: 'Just now, on that little path, my heart was pounding. I should have felt happy, but instead I was nervous. You mustn't laugh at me. You mustn't.'

'I've been nervous since the day in Canada when I booked my flights,' I say. 'I couldn't imagine how much our looks could have changed. I was afraid that we might not even recognise each other. But Madam, twenty years' time has not left a single mark on your face.'

'Not a single mark? I'm almost past middle age now. My first child is already eighteen years old.' Sister puts one arm around the girl with the beautiful teeth, saying: 'This is Xu Qian-Qian, my second child. She and Tao Yi-De are in the same class.'

Upon inspection, her eyes and brow are indeed slightly reminiscent of Sister. 'Uncle Chen,' she says, 'Mum often mentions you admiringly; we've all heard so many good things about you! Everyone wants to meet you and talk with you. Mum says, in all the classes she has been in charge of, you were the most capable, the most hardworking, and the handsomest Class Leader ever. It's a pleasure to meet you.'

'Xu Qian-Qian, aren't you laying it on a bit thick? What does that leave us, then?' Tao Yi-De asks, in all seriousness, provoking a bout of laughter.

Meanwhile, Brother-in-Law comes forward, tilts his heels, and says: 'Welcome, Mrs Wu. This is the first time you've visited the pottery workshop. No preparation has been made. It's rather untidy inside. I'm sorry about that.'

* * *

We seat ourselves on the ground, around the bonfire.

Spread over the sandy ground, over the horsetail trees, the white popinacs, the isles far and near, and over the surface of the sea, the silvery sheen of the moon renders the world as luminous as it is at sunrise. I gaze upon those 'straight-mouthed clay pots', which embrace either side of the sea, and upon Penghu Bay, which—unruffled as a lake—is shimmering with moonlight. But my heart is not unruffled.

'Glasses, what has made you so quiet?' Lin Bin asks. 'Tell us how you've been all these years. All of us, we want to know. But no tear jerking! Tell us the good things.'

'Truth be told, I haven't shed a single tear all these years. We moved to Vancouver upon my graduation from junior high school. The moment I stepped out of the aeroplane, I felt I had grown up. But although I wasn't on my own, I still felt—can you imagine this?—as if I had landed on a different planet: terrified, nervous, suspicious; whenever I went out, I strained my eyes to look, pricked up my ears to hear. And if I had learned anything at all, it was this: I had to adapt myself to this new world, learn the language well, and be on good terms with my blond, blue-eyed new friends. I had to face up to all this on my own. I couldn't hide in the house and expect others to comfort me, to help me.'

'The streets of Vancouver are neat, and they're vibrant. You can easily find there everything you need in your daily life. My father's coral business went very well from the beginning. We weren't too badly off. But try as I did, it was difficult to achieve peace of mind. The Rocky Mountains near Vancouver, the Pacific Ocean, and the Canadian Prairies—the landscapes there are vast and immensely beautiful. And I knew I was to live there for a long time—I knew I should try my best to love my new home. But deep in my heart, I was always reminiscing about this: the wind in my old hometown Penghu, the tides in Penghu Bay, the streets of Magong, the distant figures of us squatting as usual while we were chatting, eating, and watching ships in the port, and—ah yes—our somewhat salty water in the wells. I couldn't forget that, could I? Funny, isn't it?'

Like a gong burnished sparklingly bright, the moon is already hanging high above Fort Xitai. The contours of Fisherman's Isle and of the Great Bridge that spans the sea are clearly visible. I take hold of the hot tea that Brother-in-Law is passing to me and take a sip. The children are busy carrying moon cakes and pumpkin vermicelli over, placing them close to my feet; and now Tao Yi-De goes back to the workshop to fetch an armful of mangos, pomelos, pineapples, and grapes, heaping them all on the ground.

'Heaping so many things in front of Uncle Chen, aren't you going too far? It looks as if you're making offerings to the Earth God,' Lin Bin says. 'Coming back from so far away, he only wants to drink more of Penghu's water. Bring him a kettle. Let him drink it slowly.'

'Glasses, how old are your children?' Chen Xiang-Zhen asks.

'My children? I'm still single, haven't got married.'

Tao Yi-De is so surprised that he sticks out his tongue: 'Seriously? Uncle Chen wants to be a Dr Monk.'

Sister drags Tao Yi-De to her, tells him to behave himself, and asks him to sit down quietly. But that's demanding too much of him. He orders Xu Qian-Qian and the other children to get more dry wood. They all scamper away to the seaside like a wind.

'Chen Xiang-Zhen is running a holiday resort business on the Isle of Jibei. She's the manager. It's right on that coral sand beach on the northeast corner, where the archaeology team was excavating the Song and Yuan Dynasty pottery. She's built more than ten freestanding wooden cabins,' Touch-Me-Not says. 'Do you remember our trip there?'

'Of course I do.'

'Oh yes, you'll want to know this. Touch-Me-Not's cousin, who was good at Shaolin boxing—remember that kung-fu boy who could do boxing, and biting too?—he got a degree in history at National Taiwan University and came back last year to teach at Jibei Junior High School,' Chen Xiang-Zhen says. 'Yesterday I saw him bringing a group of students to a peanut field near the bronze bell, digging holes there, and saying they were doing archaeological research.'

'And he was taught by that professor, Professor Song,' Touch-Me-Not chuckles and says. 'Don't think he's still as badly behaved, as mischievous as he was. He's a specialist now, a brain-box through and through. Hard to imagine, isn't it?'

Now Tao Yi-De orders his friends to carry the television outside. It's such a bumpy journey that they nearly smash it onto the ground. 'We were talking so much that we'd forgotten about the time. The special programme has been on for quite some time. I wonder whether Uncle Pan has finished his song,' he says. 'We're not keeping up with this.'

But the figure on the television screen is none other than A-Pan. He's dressed in white from head to foot: white shoes, white trousers, a white coat with folded sleeves, and even his necktie is white. He radiates a handsome glamour, full of confidence. But as soon as we've caught a glimpse of him, he bows and walks off the stage.

'It's over. He's finished. It must be. Why else would he walk away the instant we saw him?' Lin Bin is very disappointed.

But no sooner has Lin Bin spoken than A-Pan makes his appearance again.

His new apparel makes our eyes brighten: he looks like a ferryman, wearing a Chinese shirt and baggy trousers.

'Dear audience, now I'm going to sing a new song, a song dedicated to people in my hometown of Penghu and to my dear friends—twenty years ago we promised to come back tonight for a reunion. I'd like to say: "May we be blessed with longevity, so we may share this beautiful moon, albeit a thousand miles apart",'* A-Pan looks at us and says. 'This song is called *Again I See the Gaillardias*.'

Behind A-Pan we see a projected scene, which is a hillside ablaze with gaillardias. On the slope, too, there are cows and Laogu stonewalls. A graceful A-Pan stands there, at ease with himself, singing:

---

* From a poem by the Song Dynasty poet Su Shi.

The sapphire sky broods over
    A knot of small, small isles;
Tens of thousands at a glance,
    Gaillardias blaze in bloom.
Comes the south wind, goes the north,
    Should these too be forgotten?
The footprints of our youthful days
    On the fields of golden blooms.
The deep blue sea, it fondly hugs
    A knot of small, small isles;
Tens of thousands at a glance
    Gaillardias blaze in bloom.
Comes the Kuroshio, goes the Oyashio, *
    Should these too be forgotten?
Oh my dearest, dearest friends,
    Over the sea we've gone a thousand miles,
But the roots that clutch, oh my own sweet home
The yellow flowers, in my dreams they bloom.
The roots that clutch, oh my own sweet home—
The yellow flowers, in my dreams they bloom.

The deeply moving voice flows on and on ever so gently, every single phrase plucking at my heartstrings and sinking into the depths of my heart; I can barely trust myself to breathe too hard.

As if they had been there listening to the song in the

---

* Ocean currents—the one warm and north-flowing, the other cold and south-flowing—in the western North Pacific Ocean.

studio, the children join the audience on the television and clap: 'He sang so beautifully. Did Uncle Pan sing in our pottery workshop when he was young?'

'He sang everyday. Everyday he sang. I was his top backing vocalist. Now you're impressed, aren't you?' Lin Bin says. 'I'm not a bad singer either. Next time, if you get on my bus, I'll sing you a song. I promise, once you've heard it, you'll never forget it.'

Now at last it's Brother-in-Law's turn to speak: 'How thoughtful of A-Pan! This showed his good will—it was the most heart-warming present ever. But I too have prepared a present for each of you—a little something. I hope you'll like it.' Brother-in-Law fetches a small wooden case in both hands and slowly lifts its cover: it's a case of gaillardias, gaillardias fashioned in porcelain!

The porcelain flowers are graced with red petals, edged with yellow. The glossy brightness of the glazes makes them appear wet with dew. And there's a bar and a pin attached to the back of each flower. Such exquisite artistry—they must have absorbed so much of Brother-in-Law's thought and care.

I accept one of them with both hands, keeping it cupped there, unable to speak, to say anything, for a long, long time.

'Come. Let me put it on for you. I wonder whether you'll like it or not,' Brother-in-Law says.

I feel as if I were a warrior who, after trudging a thousand miles, comes back to the general headquarters to receive a medal; the instant the medal is put on, all the fatigue resulting from prolonged battle and all the poignancy of having survived the ravages of war vanish into thin air. 'I've been to many corners of the world and seen countless flowers, but I still love gaillardias most,' I tell Brother-in-Law.

'It's unfair. Only they get to have one. What about us?' Xu Qian-Qian asks. 'Such a beautiful souvenir—we don't qualify, even if we're rich.'

'In twenty years, if you come back for a reunion, I'll give you a present too.' Brother-in-Law stands on a block of Laogu stone and asks in his deep voice: 'Will you come back for a reunion in twenty years, everyone?'

At this, Tao Yi-De says: 'Dad, that'll be 2006, in the twenty-first century. We've got to wait for a long, long time!'

Ye Ying-San accepts a porcelain gaillardia on A-Pan's behalf, intending to keep it for him until he comes back to Penghu. I pick up the last flower in the wooden case, saying: 'I'll deliver this to Fo Guang Shan in person.'

Staring at me, Chen Xiang-Zhen says: 'Glasses! …' She can't control herself; her eyes are growing wet. Touch-Me-Not hastens to join in: 'That's only right. After all, we were all classmates. This is a memorial of our youthful days. Buddhist monks and nuns are wary of mental obstructions. But are all memorials distractions? Monks and nuns, after all, are humans too—they're not Buddhas. Ah! The smoke from the bonfire is making my eyes water. Come, come. Let's try to sing A-Pan's song.'

'Glasses, can you spend a few more days in Penghu? I'll show you around,' Ye Ying-San says. 'Come to our Jibei Seaside Resort. We'll talk through the night. I'd like to hear your thoughts regarding Penghu's future development. We need your advice. You mustn't keep things to yourself. You must open up yourself, lay bare your mind.'

'Alright, I will!'

'How many batches of students have taken pottery lessons here before us, the cream of the crop?' Tao Yi-De asks Brother-in-Law.

'Twenty,' his father answers with a smile. 'And do you really think you're the cream of the crop?'

'Very well. In twenty years, I'll become a distinguished elder like Uncle Chen.' Tao Yi-De asks again: 'Dad, why is it always seven people that you choose?'

Brother-in-Law puts an arm around his shoulders. The flickering light of the bonfire dances upon the face of everyone. We begin to sing A-Pan's new song. The 'cream of the crop', the 'distinguished elder', etc.—that characteristic hauteur and flippancy in the mind of the young, in fact they conceal a larger proportion of self-ridicule and wavering; they carry a serious weight but simultaneously gesture towards a lack of confidence. In the rush to grow up as soon as possible, who doesn't discover at the same time a deep attachment to the days of one's youth? Back then, didn't we, the seven of us, go through exactly the same thing?

Epilogue

At Magong Airport, the Boeing 737 turns into the runway, runs forward, raises its nose, and takes off into the blue sky.

With my forehead pressed against the windowpane, I cast my eyes over the world below: Magong Airport, a cluster of three or four stone houses, three or four cows ambling, those Laogu wind-fences that spill out over the yellow earth on the hillsides, and files of horsetail trees and white popinacs—all of them shrinking fast. I strain my eyes to search for our pottery workshop: they said they would wave at me from the roof!

I can't find them. I can't see them. The aeroplane tilts sideways and turns, and I can only see a hillside blooming with gaillardias. 'Look, there are gaillardias everywhere,' I tell the passenger sitting next to me.

He cranes his neck and laughs: 'You have such sharp eyes, Sir. We're as high as three thousand feet in the air, and you can still see flowers?'

But I really can see them, and very clearly too.

The aeroplane is forever climbing, nose pointing towards the north. Again I press my face against the oval windowpane and look back, closely, at the sixty-four islands in the sea. They put me in mind of a necklace: aragonite beads, laid out on a blue velvet cloth, sparkling, sparkling.*

The passenger next to me asks: 'Sir, was it the first time you'd visited Penghu? Come back again and you won't be quite so dazzled.'

'Actually I'm from Penghu.'

He goggles in surprise: 'From Penghu? Seriously? Then why are you looking so closely?'

'Because I'm from Penghu.'

Over the past two days, Ye Ying-San has kept me company on a tour of Fisherman's Isle and the isles of Tongpan, Bazhao, and Qimei.

On the Isle of Jibei, we spoke long and hard. And we felt even more certain than ever that Penghu's unimproved 'wildness' is what is most precious about the place, what represents the most valuable resource it has for the future. The sunshine here, the air and the unique topographical formations here, through proper planning, will lend themselves to the creation of a perfect place for visitors to unwind and recover themselves. But what Ye Ying-

---

* Penghu is famous for aragonite crystals.

San and I pondered over and over most of all was how to preserve Penghu's distinctive features in the very process of development, so that visitors—in addition to feeling warmly welcomed and enjoying themselves—might also learn to love Penghu, to cherish Penghu. No simple matter, it was a critical manifesto and a tough challenge to boot.

A flight attendant is handing out drinks. Catching sight of the porcelain gaillardia on my shirt, her eyes light up. 'Such a beautiful brooch.' She walks towards the rear of the plane but then makes her way back again. 'Would you do a swap with me? Your brooch for my necktie?' I shake my head. 'It's a wonder drug. It works for my homesickness. I have to keep it with me at all times, never lose sight of it.'

'You're so funny,' she says, and smiles. 'Next flight, I'll go and pick one for myself.'

I don't believe she'll ever manage that. Outside the oval window, I see again—I really do—myriads of gaillardias on the undulating hillsides, two or three cows ambling there, and on a roof, a knot of people are waving at me. I know who they are. I know.

Translator's Acknowledgements

Thanks are due to the *National Museum of Taiwan Literature* for funding the work of this translation. I am grateful to Jhu Jian-Tai—the author Li Tong's widow—for her encouragement and permission to translate the novel. The translation has benifited from Peter Dale, to whom I owe my gratitude.